DARK FAE CURSED

BROKEN COURT BOOK ONE

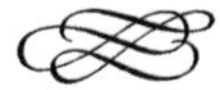

HEATHER RENEE

ISBN: 979-8685935038

Development Editing: ALD Professional Editing Services, LLC

Line Editing and Proofing: Jamie from Holmes Edits

Cover: Covers by Juan

CONTENTS

DEDICATION

For Jaymin and all of the TimTams she sends me.
Without those biscuits, I wouldn't be where I am today.
Okay, fine. And also because of you and the big heart you try
to hide.
You are the peanut butter to my jelly!

CHAPTER 1

When I'd left my high-rise apartment, all I wanted to do was get some air while waiting on news from the witches. That was it. Instead, the pondering thoughts of my future were rudely interrupted by the screams of a human as I traversed the less traveled streets of downtown Los Angeles.

I cocked my head to the side, pushing my long strands out of my face and trying to decide if I was in the mood for drama. I really wasn't, given that I had my own issues to deal with. So, I kept walking along the cracked sidewalk, switching back to my previous dilemmas until the incessant cries of the woman broke through my thoughts once more.

"Wh-what are you?" the female stuttered, the slight breeze carrying her words closer to me.

A growl echoed through the deserted streets. I sighed. Gods, I hated supernaturals who preyed on weak humans. We had a pecking order—an unwritten law—that most supernaturals abided by, but this one clearly didn't like to follow the rules. I was going to have to do something about that.

With purposeful strides, I crossed the single-lane street, flipping off the driver who honked at me. He should be thanking me for using my invaluable time to save one of his kind.

A streetlight flickered above the brick alleyway, but I couldn't see much and continued to follow the moans and grunts behind a dumpster.

The female human was on the trash-filled ground, curled in the fetal position, while a scraggly grey wolf nipped at her ankles, merely playing with his food. Idiot mutt.

Magic gathered in my hand, and I flicked a stream of it right at his tail, singeing half the hair off. "Didn't your mother teach you not to play with your food?" I drawled.

The young woman's hazel eyes widened at my appearance, and her fair skin became almost translucent behind the thin curtain of ebony hair.

Unfortunately, I made the rookie mistake of watching the prey instead of keeping my focus on the wolf. He lunged for me, claws scratching my arm, but that was the only hit he'd be allowed. I flicked my wrist once more, sending a stream of power at his chest that acted like electricity, and didn't let up until I smelled burnt hair.

He fell over onto his side, looking more like an oversized house-dog than the badass shifter he should have been. After a couple of growls, his form shimmered, but I had no desire to argue with a rogue. I blasted him with another bout of magic, stopping his shift.

Bending closer to the ground, I snapped my fingers to get his full attention. "I don't think so, furball. No shifting back to human form until you're long gone from this territory. You clearly don't belong to any of the local packs, so run along now before I kill you instead."

Don't give him the option. Just kill him now before he becomes a bigger problem. Ah, my inner darkness had decided to come out and play. Well, I wasn't in the mood. Instead, I ignored that voice and took a step back from the mangy shifter, groaning at the blood I'd dripped on my favorite high heels.

His jowls snapped at me, foam forming along his jaw while his beady black eyes narrowed.

Power pooled in my hand once more, and I let my own growl out. "I don't give second chances. Go now or die."

He yipped as the power of my words slammed into him, then rolled in the opposite direction before jumping over the woman who was still on the ground. The wolf limped along before using the dumpster to launch himself over the fence and disappearing into the night.

"Who are you?" she muttered, snot running down her nose.

"Nobody you'll remember," I replied, ready to make her forget this whole incident.

More tears streamed down her face as she sat up and reached to hug me. "You're my hero."

My head shook as my palm went to her forehead. "Honey, I'm the furthest thing from a hero. I just hate bullies. Now, you're going to forget this happened, and I'm never going to see you again."

My hand stayed in place as I pushed magic into her mind. I couldn't do this trick on other supernaturals, but I certainly took advantage of it with the feeble minds of humans when necessary.

She mumbled incoherently as I stepped away into the shadows and waited until she stood, crying at the sight of her torn clothes and bruises. Hopefully, she'd figure out the situation wasn't as bad as it first appeared.

Once she was gone, I left the alley and finished the trek home. A quick glance at my phone told me Neva was due back any minute. I was going to need a shower after that interlude. Blood wasn't something I enjoyed keeping on my skin, and while my wound was healed with my accelerated fae healing, the mess wouldn't go away on its own.

I should have just taken my Ferrari for a spin when I needed to get out. This was part of my problem. I'd been "helping" around this territory for much too long. I was growing complacent, or maybe soft. I wasn't sure which. Either way, I didn't like it. My actions were beginning to allow emotions in that I'd fought hard to avoid for many years.

I'd learned long ago that caring would give me nothing but heartache.

King Zephyr stood in my room, holding a doll I'd been given by a complete stranger as a child. The only real gift I'd ever been given. "You showed weakness today. You didn't kill the fae, and now they'll think they can get away with disobeying me. That displeases me, Lucinda."

"I'm sorry, Zephy. I'll do better next time." I was only fourteen. Even though I looked like an adult, I was still a child.

"Let this be your punishment." He tore the head from my doll, throwing both halves into the fireplace in my room. "I need you strong. You can't care about those other fae. They mean nothing to you. I'm all you need."

Gods, I'd been so naïve. Even though I knew better now, I still had my issues. A part of me wondered if a change of scenery would get me out of this funk, but I'd been hard-pressed to give up the high-rise apartment I'd swindled out of some movie executive who'd been unfaithful to his wife. Not with me, of course. I didn't date humans, but I had been all too happy to dole out his punishment and get something for myself out of it. I had one of the witch covens to thank for that job.

I'd come to Earth three years ago and had managed to make the best out of things after being kicked out of Fae Islands by King Easton Zephyr. At one time, I'd been his favorite guard, but the king's loyalty was only skin deep, and one misperception was all it took for the bastard to turn on me. Even though the islands were my home, I had zero desire to ever set foot on them again.

Instead, I'd come to Earth and chose to begin working with the shifters and witches. The two races typically despised each other, but I'd managed to play them like a fiddle. When one had a problem with the other—or any supernatural race for that matter—that they couldn't solve on their own, they called on me to handle the situation.

Torturing those who deserved it helped to feed the darkness that stirred inside me—that inner voice that pushed me to be worse than I was the day before. Normally, I didn't mind using my darker subconscious as a crutch, but lately, something was missing. Though, I hadn't figured out what that was.

My only rule was that I never messed with kids. If there was ever the slightest chance a child could get hurt, I'd tell whoever was requesting my services to piss off, or, depending on how twisted the situation was, I turned their request back on them.

Sometimes supernaturals needed to be knocked down from their pedestal, and I was always happy to oblige.

It had been that way ever since I was a child. I learned early on that bullies needed to be taught lessons, but there wasn't always someone around to do so. That was when I decided to be that person.

Right before the previous fae queen died and her brother—the current king—took over, she'd given my parents a falcon as a gift. Weeks passed, and I'd witnessed the predator bird terrorize the other wild animals in our area who, as a young fae, I'd considered friends.

At the age of nine, I'd been so sure I knew right from wrong. The bird had needed to go.

But my parents had thought otherwise, and I was the one who paid the price.

They'd been furious when I'd cut its head off and hadn't believed me when I said it was only in defense. My penance? They sold me to the king in exchange for another damn bird.

That was nine years ago, and I'd spent five of those years being turned into something I wasn't sure I should be proud of. Regardless, I'd accepted who I was, never once regretting how my life turned out.

Sure, once I'd been banished, I could have reformed, but even at fifteen, I knew in my soul it was too late to really make a difference. I was who I was, and I'd accepted it long ago.

The only thing I let myself care about was punishing those who deserved my wrath. It was the only way to rein in the darkness I carried. It was my way of repenting for all the wrongs I'd been forced to do by the king without having to face the actual consequences of my previous actions.

"Neva," I called out when I arrived back at my apartment, hoping she'd returned before me.

"Yes, Ms. Morrow?" My faithful assistant's form shimmered into appearance and began following me while I continued to walk toward my room, stripping off my bloodied clothes along the way.

I sighed. "When will you quit being so formal?"

"I'm sorry, Ms. Lucinda."

Well, that was at least better than using the last name I didn't care for.

"Lucy also works, you know?" I added, but she merely smiled at me, and I knew I needed to let it go. For now, at least.

Neva was a rare brownie elf. Poor thing had been a hideous mess before I stumbled upon her two years ago being beaten by a group of young cubs that I'd let live per Neva's begging. Though, I'd made sure I would be starring in their nightmares for the rest of their lives before I was through with them.

In exchange for saving her life and revealing her true beauty with my fae magic, she'd offered to stick around and help me with whatever I might need. At the time, I couldn't think of a single reason why I needed her—by then, I'd already accepted being alone was best —but she quickly showed me how essential she could be, and I grew used to her company.

Once I entered my bedroom, I relieved myself of every stitch of clothing, even though it had only been my shirt to get blood on it. Neva flinched at my lack of attire, but I had no qualms about standing before her naked. Along with being unable to break her from using formalities, she still hadn't adjusted to my crass ways.

I held my hand out. "My robe?"

Brownie elves made the best assistants.

"Here you are, Ms. Lucinda." Neva magicked my silk black wrap into appearance, and I covered myself. I wasn't a complete monster. I just liked to push the boundaries. A lot. But intentions were good when it came to Neva. One of these days, I'd unearth the strong elf I saw lying behind all her formalities.

"I need to shower the stench of wolf off me, but first, what did the witches want?" I asked.

Her honey eyes stared up at me. Eyes that had been

dull and lifeless when she met me were now filled with hope, and I wasn't sure which was worse. The elf was nearly a foot shorter than me. Though, what she lacked in height, I'd made sure she compensated for in strength and looks after I'd given her a boost of magic.

Her skin was smooth and tinted a deep umber. She had a round face that helped her innocence shine through and also came in handy when she did my bidding. People seemed to trust Neva, and that made the brownie elf even more useful, considering very few trusted a dark fae like me.

"The coven first mentioned that you're upsetting the balance and causing the humans to be irrational when you lure them in and take what you want. They ask if you wouldn't mind limiting your punishing to the other supernaturals before they're forced to clean up a mess you can't. Their words, not mine, of course."

"I thought they called for me because they had a *real* issue, not a complaint." I knew my stay on Earth was a tenuous one. I knew I was pushing the buttons of the other supernaturals that called this place home, but I had a strange curiosity and couldn't help myself. Plus, Los Angeles had grown on me. At least, I had thought so until recently.

"Well, they do have an issue with a vampire."

Glee filled me within an instant. Beating on the wolf hadn't been enough to quench the darkness within me, and it had been nearly two weeks since my last real outing. Given how antsy I'd been getting, this one was coming at the perfect time. I had even been letting thoughts of moving consume me.

The wolf could have been enough if you'd just killed it.

I ignored the inner comment and turned to Neva. "Perfect. Let me shower and we'll be on our way." Then, I sauntered to my bathroom, but Neva cleared her throat. "Yes?" I said without turning around.

"Don't you want to know what they want with the vampire and who he is?"

Slowly, I swiveled my head back toward her. "I assume they want him dead, and does it really matter who he is? I've done business with Beatrix before. She knows my conditions. I doubt she'd risk my wrath by requesting me to harm someone who didn't deserve it." Plus, the bloodsuckers were my least favorite of all the supernaturals. I was going to enjoy torturing this one.

Her fingers twisted together with obvious nerves. "Well, he's an older vampire, and Beatrix doesn't want him dead. She merely wants him as a prisoner to the coven."

My brow arched. Maybe I was interested. "To do what with?"

"They didn't say."

Hmm. While I enjoyed a good kill and could really use it to calm my inner being, the challenge of capturing might not be too bad as long as he was strong.

I was also interested in why an all-female coven wanted a male vampire as their prisoner. I could certainly imagine the things they had planned for him.

"Very well. It doesn't change anything. Now, I really need to shower." My nose turned up. "Remind me to just go to the rooftop next time I want some air."

"Yes, Ms. Lucinda." Neva disappeared, all too eager to give me my privacy while I got ready.

A glance at the clock showed it was after midnight and the perfect time to go vampire hunting. They'd be out preying on the drunks leaving the clubs, and I could use their lust for blood against them. Even though bloodsuckers were lightning fast and nearly immortal, the fact that blood held so much power over them made the vampires one of our weaker species, in my opinion.

I moved to get in the shower, but my reflection caught my attention first. My normally light azure eyes had a darker ring of black around them, and if I wasn't mistaken, there was a wrinkle forming near the corner of my right eye.

Earth was literally sucking the life out of me.

As much as I didn't want to ever step back onto Fae Islands, I was beginning to wonder if I wouldn't have a choice at some point.

Pushing the worry aside, I moved my long iridescent-indigo hair to the side and ran a brush through the thick strands as I searched for more changes. My lips were still full and nose straight. My skin held its unnatural glow that the humans rarely noticed. After being around them only a short time, I'd learned their weak minds were good at ignoring what they couldn't handle.

Lastly, I drew on my magic and focused on my favorite part of the day. Calling forth my power, I made sure my hair was out of the way and let my hold go. My signature teal magic trickled from my fingertips and worked its way up my arms, wrapping around my shoulders.

My wings emerged with hardly any effort, and I sighed with relief as my true self came to life.

Some fae had gossamer wings, and others had leathery ones, but feathered ones were rare. Mine were made from the strongest feathers known to any supernatural and sharp as the finest blades in existence when I wanted them to be.

I'd only known a handful of other fae like me, but never actually met any of them in person. So, for me, my wings were one-of-a-kind. They began between my shoulder blades, pitch black in color, and as they extended out just beyond my outstretched fingertips, they changed to a charcoal hue, giving my wingspan an ombre effect.

My teal magic reflected off the hard edges of my pointed tips, and I let my undamaged robe fall to the ground. The feathers were magically capable of sliding through whatever material might be in their way to freedom.

Pulling my wings closer, they wrapped around my torso, holding me tight and providing me with a sense of security I couldn't get from anywhere else.

I closed my eyes, soaking in the power for several minutes before drawing it back in. When I was done, I gave myself one more cursory glance and noticed the wrinkle I'd seen before was gone. My lips lifted and I turned for the shower, forgetting about my earlier worries.

It was time to hunt a vampire.

CHAPTER 2

After I was dried off from my shower, I dressed in a leather corset, dark blue jeans, and my favorite black heeled boots before taking a peek in the mirror one last time. My plan included making the vampire think I was searching for a good time, so I could entice him with little fuss.

Vampires might be weak to their needs, but unfortunately, they weren't stupid. Everything about me needed to be perfect.

Using my hands, I adjusted my cleavage then puffed up my hair and headed to the door. Neva was waiting for me, also dressed to the nines, which surprised me. "Are you coming with me?"

Normally, she only organized my outings and didn't participate in them, but if she wanted to expand her usefulness, I was more than happy to let her watch a master at work.

"Something about tonight doesn't feel right. I know you're capable of handling yourself, but I'd like to be close by in case you need me." Neva's thick ebony curls bounced around her cherub face.

"Just don't get yourself bitten by a bloodsucker." I tossed a wink her way before walking through the front door. Instead of having her give more info at the house, she could do it on the way.

While I enjoyed pushing Neva past her comfort zone, I had a lot of respect for her as another supernatural and hoped one day she'd be able to thank me for being the person in her life that didn't let her lay down and be bullied by the monsters of our world. She might have been decades older than me, but I'd been through hell and grown up much faster than any other supernatural I knew.

When we reached the elevator, I entered my code for the garage and turned toward the glass windows of the enclosure to take in the city. The moon was high in the sky, but with the light pollution, there wasn't a single star visible. My apartment sat on top of one of the most prestigious buildings in LA on Wilshire Boulevard, and nearly everyone here valued their privacy.

Neva stayed quiet, even as we exited the elevator and walked the few spaces until Black Widow came into view. My fingers traced over her sleek lines until Neva tossed me the keys. The car was my pride and joy. I loved her even more than my high-rise apartment.

She was a Ferrari 488 Spider and worth every moment I spent torturing the sleazy car dealership owner. I'd witnessed him treat his teen son like shit because he wanted to try out for the school musical instead of the football team. When I was done with him,

I'd not only gotten a new car, but the kid was enrolled in acting classes.

I slid into the plush leather seat that hugged my body perfectly and waited for Neva to do the same before starting the car. I pressed my thumb against the ignition, then enjoyed the vibrations as over six hundred horsepower roared to life. Gods, I loved this car.

"It's like a wet dream, isn't it?" I grinned at Neva.

She grimaced but indulged me with a nod anyway.

"Where did the witches say we'd find this vampire, and what do I need to know about him?" I asked over the purr of the motor as I drove out of my parking space.

The elf took her phone out and read the screen. "Beatrix said he usually hangs out at Warlock and his name is Dante. Here's a picture of him."

I soaked in every detail of the image. His brunet hair and golden skin were a stark contrast to his dark, ominous eyes set just above a pointed, yet slightly crooked, nose. Probably from putting it where it didn't belong. There was even a faint scar above his right eye. This guy was definitely scrappy. Even better for me.

While I couldn't deny he was alluring even just from a picture—probably the bad boy vibe calling to me—I wouldn't have thought he was worth the trouble of capturing alive. Then again, I didn't like to ask too many questions. As long as the request didn't check one of my hard-no boxes, I rarely ever second-guessed my assignments. The pay days were usually worth it, too, ranging from money to extravagant items, like my high-rise apartment, all the way to magical favors owed.

"We haven't been to Warlock for fun in a while. Maybe we can have a drink while we're there," I said to Neva once I was done taking in the bloodsucker. She hadn't been to the club on business with me, but I'd taken her several times just to loosen her up.

"Just don't mess with the celebrities until *after* we're done with the vampire." Neva replied with a sigh, likely remembering the last time we were at the ritzy club that was merely nicknamed Warlock by supernaturals and was where the magically enhanced celebrities liked to let loose.

It wasn't a coincidence that Chris Hemsworth was perfect for the role of Thor. Everything about him was supernaturally superior, and I meant *everything*.

"You have a little drool on your chin, Ms. Lucinda." Neva smirked as if she knew exactly what I was thinking.

Surprisingly, traffic was light, and we arrived at Warlock in record time. The valet took my keys, his eyes unable to stray from my chest, and I tapped him on the nose with a shock of magic. "Enjoy them all you want."

The young kid blushed, eyes bright with my power as he muttered an apology, then slipped into the car without another word or longing gaze.

"Did you forget about the part where the witches asked you to stop messing with the humans, Ms. Lucinda?" Neva asked as I joined her on the sidewalk and skipped the line, but I ignored the question. It was time to play my part.

Gregory, the beast of a man who guarded the entrance, gave me a once-over. "Lucy, it's been a while." He glanced at his watch. "And you're here earlier than normal. Leaves more time for trouble."

I offered a sultry smile. "I know, but I just have a quick thing inside, and I won't cause a scene."

He grimaced. "That's what you said last time."

"But I promise this time. In and out, like I was never even here." Sometimes I preferred to use force and magic to get what I wanted, and other times it was suitable to simply make acquaintances. I knew the moment I stepped into LA two years ago that it was going to be my home—the hotel-hopping could only work for so long. So, while I'd caused some commotions here and there with the humans, I'd also managed to make some allies along the way.

He rubbed a hand over his bald head. "Alright, go on in."

Pulling a hundred from my corset, I ran the edges of the bill down his cheek before tucking it into the pocket of his silk shirt. "You're the best, Gregory."

His light skin blushed as he moved the rope out of the way and allowed us in. Others still in line complained, but he yelled at them to shut it, and I grinned. I'd made the right call when adding a club bouncer to my list of people I liked.

Neva took in the heavy atmosphere of alcohol and sexual tension with a dash of magic while I searched the booths and couches for the mark. Half of the club was filled with humans and the other half with supernaturals. Ignoring those who didn't give off a magical presence, my eyes traveled around the dimly lit room. I caught glimpses of a few witches, several shifters, and a handful of vampires, but not the one from the picture.

A waitress walked up to us, carrying a tray of empty glasses. "Would you like me to find you a table, Ms. Morrow?"

I waved my hand dismissively. "No, we're not ready to sit just yet."

Her face scrunched in confusion, but I didn't have time to explain myself to a human who wouldn't understand anyway. I grabbed on to Neva's hand and pulled her toward the bar where we wouldn't stand out so much. "Stay close to me. Once we spot him, this should move quickly."

Even under the dim lights, I could see her eyes widen and knew she was already overwhelmed. She could wrangle supernaturals on a smaller scale just fine when organizing my assignments, but being crammed into a building with a couple hundred people and pulsing music was a different story.

Wind blew across my neck, and my indigo hair brushed across my shoulder. There were no open windows in the club that I'd spotted, and no fans graced the ceiling above me, which left me to believe someone was using magic.

I searched the area, not only for the vampire, but for anyone paying too much attention to us. Nothing stood out, and the bar was still devoid of one vampire named Dante. A growl of frustration built in my chest.

If I was a dirty bloodsucker looking for an easy mark, where would I be?

Neva tugged on my hand. "What's in the back corner over there?"

I followed where she nodded and saw there was a new addition to the club since I'd last been. "Stay here. I'll be right back."

The elf didn't argue, but also didn't take her eyes off me as I moved through the crowd. A man approached me when I was halfway to the exit. "Hey there, sugar."

I was pretty sure he meant to purr the words, but instead his voice was obnoxiously low with an irritating wheeze.

"Not tonight, fleabag."

He grabbed my arm. "Oh, come on, sweetheart. You didn't come here dressed like that to go home alone."

I moved closer and lowered my voice. "If you want to keep your hand and balls, I suggest you let go of me right the hell now. And if I catch you harassing another woman because she felt the need to dress up for a fun night out, I will find you, then make sure you know how it feels to be the victim of a predator."

His eyes glazed over in fear, but he'd yet to release his hold on me. I moved in closer, wanting to make my point and move on, and grabbed the collar of his button up shirt. "If you think I'm kidding, ask Gregory about Lucy." Then, I shoved the human trash away and he stumbled to the floor, but I didn't stick around long enough to see if he got up.

Instead, I beat my darkness back into submission that the scumbag had caused to rise, once again begging me to kill. I wouldn't be ready to unleash the inner me until we had Dante in hand, so I focused back on the task of finding out what was beyond the door I could now see people moving in and out of. Once I made my way past the bumping and grinding of people, I found myself in an outside bar of sorts and wondered if that was where the wind I'd felt before had been from.

Before I could ponder too much about it, I found who I'd come for. The vampire sat in a corner with a human in his lap. Her eyes were foggy from his magic, and I knew if I didn't act soon, she'd be too much of a distraction to get his attention in the way I wanted.

They stood from their spot, and I retreated back to the door. The redhead could barely walk on her own in four-inch heels and the tight black dress she had on, but I knew that wasn't the only thing hindering her ability to stand straight.

I hadn't counted on Dante already having made his mark for the night, but it wouldn't stop me. Vampires weren't the only predator expert at luring in their prey. Plus, I'd promised Gregory I wouldn't make a scene, so it was time to see how good my corset really worked.

When the group of humans ahead of the vampire moved through the exit, I positioned myself in the doorway. With my back pressed against one side and my left leg up, I pressed my heeled boot against the frame, effectively blocking it while undoing the top button to my corset. Black lace peeked out, and I tousled my hair just enough to hopefully call attention to what I wanted Dante to believe I was offering.

I was pretending to play on my phone when a throat

cleared, but I didn't move from my post. I knew I was drawing the attention of others around us, but Dante's was the only one I was truly concerned with. I wanted him nice and riled up before I gave him my full attention.

He pushed against my foot, but it didn't budge. "Are you going to move or is being a bitch your only goal tonight?" Dante snarled with an accent I couldn't place.

I bit my lip and slowly glanced up while using one hand to tuck strands of indigo hair behind my ear. "Oh, am I in your way? Silly me." Slowly, I drew my leg down, watching Dante and confirming it was him by the scar above his eye.

Once I was back on two feet, I moved in closer, giving him the full effect of what I wanted him to think he could have by adding a little magic to the shock that flowed between us as I purposely brushed my body against his while moving out of his way.

His sharp intake of breath told me everything I needed to know. "Who are you?" he asked, barely holding on to the girl he should have been taking better care of.

Vampires were allowed to feed on the humans as long as they didn't leave a mess behind and made them forget about the experience. The majority of humans didn't know about us, and we liked it that way. At least, most of us did.

"I'm Lucy. I'm just passing through town and heard this was the place to go if I wanted to find a little fun, if you know what I mean. Looks like you've already found yours for the night. Pity." I fluttered my lashes at him, and his eyes flashed red.

He grinned seductively. "Well, I'm Dante, and this one is a regular. She's here every time I visit." He gestured to the nearly unconscious woman who was now swaying side to side. "Let me take her back, and I'll make sure your time in LA is not only fun, but pleasurable."

Shit, he was actually very good at what he did. My skin heated from his continued accent I was beginning to think originated from Italy, and I was becoming curious as to what kind of pleasure he might be able to elicit from me. No longer did I wonder why the witches wanted him alive.

If Dante was as powerful as I sensed, then he'd already be well aware of what I was. The fact that he thought I was just passing through was likely what lured him in, but little did he know, he was in for the surprise of his life.

I sent off a text to Neva, letting her know to come check on the girl as soon as we walked away. I despised collateral damage and wasn't sure what kind of vampire magic Dante was capable of. Plus, I didn't need the Supernatural Council putting their noses in my business if something happened to a human while I'd been around.

The council consisted of ten supernaturals from varying races, but mostly witches, vampires, and shifters. Their members changed every year and their identities were usually kept secret for their safety. They used supernatural hunters to investigate reports and dole out punishment, but I'd heard on rare occasions they've shown up in smaller groups to do it themselves when the situations were too sensitive to entrust to just anyone. Oh, what I would have given to watch that show.

Just as I tucked my phone into my back pocket, the bloodsucker appeared at my side. "Your place or mine?"

His dark eyes took another long moment to drink me in before I answered. "How about my hotel down the road? I drove here, and my car is in the back."

He smiled, fangs on full display, but I managed to hold in my cringe. In no way was I letting those things get near my skin. I was no vamp tramp.

Some supernaturals enjoyed the thrill of letting a bloodsucker drink from them, but it had never been my brand of adventure.

"You got it, gorgeous." He tugged me closer and took a deep inhale of my hair. "We don't see fae around here much. Trouble in paradise?"

I shook my head and grinned. "Just on holiday."

That bit of information excited him further, and I was worried the job would be too easy to satisfy the darkness within me. I'd been hoping for a challenge, yet Dante appeared to be putty in my hands. It was convenient but disappointing, considering how slow business had been.

As we moved through the back of the club, crowds parted just enough for us to walk through without bumping into everyone we passed. The natural predator vibe that exuded from Dante actually came in handy.

He held the door open to the alleyway that led to the back lot where the cars were parked, but I wouldn't be taking him in that direction. Instead, I pretended to stumble on the cobblestone alley and blushed before righting myself. "That bartender sure knows how to make a drink. Let me just text my friend that I'm leaving before you drive us."

Dante sauntered closer, his hands reaching for me, but I moved a few steps back until my screen was out of his view, and asked Neva to make sure Beatrix was ready for her toy after Neva had finished with the human. Since the elf had wanted to come along, I wanted her to feel helpful instead of just sitting inside until I was done.

I didn't wait for her reply as I slipped the phone away and gazed at Dante through hooded eyes. "I don't think I can wait until we get back to my room."

Drawing my magic forward, I reached out and tugged on the collar of his crisp white dress shirt. He didn't resist, so I took charge and pushed him against the brick wall of the alley. We were just beyond a wall of wooden pallets, mostly out of view from anyone else who might be leaving.

"Vixen," he hissed. "I had a feeling you were going to be a challenge." Using his speed, he changed our positions and my exposed shoulder blades dug into the rough surface, but I didn't let the bite of stone deter me.

"There's nothing interesting about life when it's not challenging, don't you agree?" I asked before letting him press his lips to my neck while I sank my fingers into his russet hair and released my wings. My rough hold had him growling against my skin, and the pheromones of pulsing desire he was releasing were almost enough to distract me.

Almost, but not quite.

He finally noticed my wings and paused. "You like the risk of being out here where anyone could find us, don't you? It turns you on almost as much as I do." He took another inhale. "Your arousal is the most sensual thing I've tasted in the air tonight."

Well, enough with that.

The vampire was more powerful than I'd given him credit for, and I couldn't deny he was affecting me. I needed to remember why I was there before I broke my commitment to Beatrix and let the vampire have his way with me. Something I was certain to regret in the morning.

"How about we move this along? Less words, more action," I suggested while hardening my wings and preparing to end my façade.

Only, someone else had entered the alley, and if they came any closer, they would find out what happened when they screwed with my agenda.

CHAPTER 3

Thankfully, the newcomer didn't step any closer, remaining in the shadows, and his presence didn't distract me enough to get in the way of the task at hand. Though, it was close. Whoever lurked behind the wooden crates was fae and likely from Fae Islands. Very few of us left our so-called perfect realm permanently, and I'd need to figure out his motives. Though, before I could, I focused back on the vampire who currently had his tongue running along my neck.

"Watch the fangs," I murmured, then positioned myself to the side before deciding my first move.

Not for another second could I underestimate Dante. There was a reason Beatrix asked me to take care of this particular problem for her, and I wouldn't soon forget that, even if I wasn't aware of the exact purpose.

"Ahh, but my fangs are the second-best part of me," he cooed. I ignored him, along with the desires he'd managed to induce within me.

The fae stranger inched closer, so before I had two opponents to deal with, I had to make my move on Dante.

My fingers gripped the bloodsucker's hair. He merely thought I was being rough again until I yanked his head back and slammed it into the bricks behind us.

"What the hell?" His fangs extended fully, and his previously mysterious eyes bled through with crimson.

Ignoring his outburst, I pooled magic in my palm and flung it toward his chest while he was still against the wall. Just a little something to keep him immobile until Beatrix showed up to claim her vampire, as long as she made it soon. Though, a part of me preferred she didn't. Toying with him for a little while didn't sound like the worst idea.

But Dante was faster than I'd given him credit for. My magic hadn't reached him before he whirled around me in the blink of an eye. Before I could turn around, his foot slammed into my back, right between my wings, causing them to buckle and wrap around me, throwing my weight off balance.

I fell forward and caught myself against the brick wall. I tried to suck in a deep breath, but he was already on me again. The darker part inside of me flared to life and my wings spread, glowing with a hue of teal magic.

His elongated nails dug into my wing and jerked my body around before pinning me to the wall. This time, there wasn't an ounce of sexual need, and his spell over me was broken.

"I'm going to rip your throat out," he sneered, and I

was suddenly pissed the hell off that I was supposed to keep him alive. It would have been so much easier to just cut his head off with my wingtips.

"Yeah, that's not going to happen," I replied right before I used my left elbow to slam into his jaw and my right to blast him with paralyzing magic once again, this time not missing my mark.

My powers seeped into the vampire's chest and caused him to stagger, but he recovered quicker than expected. His lips lifted as he snarled in my face and wrapped his hands around my neck.

I'd finally had enough and brought my wings forward, holding them right at his throat, ready to slice it open regardless of what Beatrix wanted. "Let go of me and I won't remove your head." My eyes narrowed and glowed as my power rose closer to the surface.

He flinched but didn't back down. One hand pushed my wing just far enough to the side that his head had enough room to slam into mine. Dante seemed uncaring that my wingtips had nearly taken his fingers off.

His impact made my nose crack, causing me to let out several choice words before my fae healing began to kick in, and Dante didn't give me a moment to recover. He went for my legs next, and my body crashed into the dirty concrete ground.

Damn, that hurt, but I was done playing around. It was time to show him who he was messing with.

"Now *this* is where you belong. Right on your back." Dante's fangs aimed for my neck as he moved in.

My wings were flat against the concrete, but I

brought them forward before his mouth could reach my skin and the hardened tops sliced clean through his left ear. He froze in place before I could continue to his neck.

Trying to keep Beatrix in mind since Neva had made a deal, I didn't immediately kill him. "Let's have some real fun," I said before driving my fist into his nose, breaking it like his marble skin did mine.

He might have been strong and given me a challenge, but he couldn't beat me, and based on the flicker of rage in his eyes, he realized it, too.

"Screw you." He spat blood and was lucky he missed my face.

"Awe, you're not going to be *that* fortunate tonight, vampy." Wasting no more time, I put my final moves into motion.

My wings pulled back—still attempting to keep him mostly in one piece for Beatrix—and I hooked my left leg around his while I pushed on his chest with both hands, slamming power into his core.

My magic had a visible effect this time, and the darker voice within me sung like a church choir. That was what I'd needed. This sex-on-a-stick deserved to have his ass handed to him, and I was glad to be the one to do it.

A wave of new magic entered the alleyway, so I wasted no time getting one last hit in, this time adding a bit of something special that would keep the vampire down for at least an hour. Enough time for the witch to get him wherever she needed.

"Neva," I called out just once, and she appeared immediately. "Is that Beatrix I sense?"

The elf nodded at the same time the witch walked out of the shadows, a trail of fog behind her. I was interested in why she hid herself, but not enough to ask. Instead, I was ready to be done with Dante before I accidentally killed him and enraged an entire coven.

"I'd heard you were good, but I must say, I'm a little disappointed." Beatrix tsked, and I instantly wanted to slice her in two. "You made that look too easy," she added a second later, saving me the trouble of killing her *and* the vamp.

"Well, it is what you hired me for," I replied with bite in my voice, still kneeling over Dante. Even if she hadn't meant to insult me, she'd still struck a nerve and needed to know. Though, I wasn't sure if my short temper had more to do with her or the fae that still lingered where he didn't belong.

"Do you need me to transport him to your coven?" I asked, curious to see what she had behind the walls of the compound she kept so guarded.

She stared down at me and flicked her silver braid behind her shoulder, emerald eyes sparking with plenty of life even though the wrinkles around her face made her seem elderly. "Not a chance in hell, but I do owe you. Would you like payment now or later?"

I considered the fae behind me while Dante still struggled against my spell underneath me. There was a chance I'd need to ditch the newcomer, depending on what he wanted. I couldn't risk killing a fae and bringing more problems to my doorstep, in case he was someone important to the fae realm. Asking for something so simple wasn't usually my kind of payment, though it would do this time.

"How about a spell?" I requested.

She raised a brow. "That's it? What kind?"

Instead of answering her, I sat up to pull my phone from my back pocket and groaned at the cracked screen. I'd need Neva to fix it. Her repair skills far surpassed mine, but regardless of the damage, the apps still worked as I pulled up my notes and typed in my request.

She squinted as I held it up. "You expect me to read that? What's wrong with talking?"

"Just indulge me, will you?" I sighed, clearly over tonight after dealing with the annoying werewolf, then a vampire who'd made me sexually frustrated.

I passed her the phone again and waited not-so-patiently until she glanced back at me. "That's simple enough. Do you want it now or shall I make it to go?"

"To go would be preferable. I have some more business to handle before I go home." I said the last part a little louder than necessary, so the fae would know I was aware of his presence. When he still didn't leave, I knew there was no avoiding dealing with him before I could get some sleep.

"Very well." Beatrix dug into the deep pockets of the loose overcoat she wore and pulled out a vial with clear liquid. Her palms covered the glass, and she murmured into them, causing sparks to flicker around her fingertips.

While she was busy with that, I leaned forward and

pulsed an extra dose of magic into Dante just for fun. "Look at you being a good little vampire and staying still."

His eyes were pure crimson now, and I enjoyed the inner turmoil showcasing in his face. Something told me he'd never been bested by a woman. I stood, leaving my wings on display, and brushed myself off as well as possible while Beatrix finished the spell.

When she was done inspecting her work, I held my hand out until she dropped the vial into my palm. "It's been a pleasure doing business with you," she said.

Before I bothered to respond, Beatrix knelt down and placed a hand on Dante whose skin had begun to smoke as he attempted to fight against my power with his own, but it was pointless. He was only going to get himself killed by doing so, and I had no doubt the witches were going to have their fun with the vamp.

We should be enjoying the catch. Not them, my inner voice snarled.

Apparently, our little fight had only scratched the surface of my needs.

Beatrix waved goodbye and disappeared with her prize, making me glad the bloodsucker was no longer my problem. Maybe the loitering fae could help satisfy the inner darkness that was storming inside me.

Neva stepped closer to me, but I put a hand up. "How about you go get Black Widow?"

Her jaw dropped. "You want *me* to drive Black Widow?"

"If you wouldn't mind. I just need to check on one

last thing before we can go home." Or possibly kill one last thing if I didn't have a choice, but that was a detail she didn't need to know.

Her eyes scanned the area, and even though Neva was resourceful and good at assisting, she wasn't created to be a predator like I was. She wouldn't sense the fae. Not unless he wanted her to.

"Okay, so I'll pull the car back here after I get the keys, then?" she asked for confirmation, and I nodded.

Hopefully, I could handle whatever the fae wanted quickly and then be done with him. I hadn't had an interaction with another of my kind in years. I preferred it that way, too. Ever since the king turned on me—for saving his life, no less—I'd chosen my own path.

When I'd worked for the king, I was a guard and went on missions whenever told. Sure, I'd punished people then, but it was different. I was young and naïve. I'd considered anything the king said to be truth and bowed before him without question.

Now? Now, I knew better. I still got the bad guys for others too lazy to do it themselves, like Beatrix, but it was more for my benefit than anyone else's. I needed the release like I needed the air to breathe. I needed the redemption for the person the king had turned me into. The tasks I did on Earth were the only things that kept me from completely losing my shit and storming Fae Islands to demand vengeance.

There had been days, though… some dark fucking days when I plotted King Zephyr's death over and over again like a true psychopath.

Once Neva was gone from the alleyway, I shook the dark thoughts away, and the fae stepped from the shadows enough that I could see his silhouette under the flickering light. Though, not enough to make out the details of his face.

My wings stretched further, and their hardened tips glinted under the dim light. I wanted him to know exactly who he was dealing with before he even got the chance to speak.

"What do you want?" I asked, hands ready for a fight at my sides. This one I didn't *have* to leave alive, but I'd try, merely to avoid any drama his death could cause.

"I need a favor." His voice was husky and strained, as if asking for help was the hardest thing he'd ever had to do.

"Why would I help you?" I countered, curious about his stiff composure.

He inched forward. "You wouldn't. It's not me I'm here for. It's my sister. I've heard it's what you do. That you're the best at freeing people from adverse situations."

Instead of responding, I took a moment to appraise him, trying to read between the lines and figure out what he wasn't saying.

He was tall, likely close to seven feet, given the height he had on my nearly six-foot frame. His muscles stood out beneath the tight white shirt that clung to his skin, and I was surprised he didn't have his wings out.

Maybe his were the gossamer kind and he was

embarrassed. I smirked as I visualized him looking more like a fairy than the fae warrior his muscles hinted at, muscles that made my tongue dart out to wet my lips.

His silver eyes flashed with unfiltered rage. "What's funny?"

"Just my imagination. Now, what is it that you think I can help your sister with?"

"She needs to have a spell removed from her," he replied through gritted teeth.

My head cocked to the side. There was something about this fae that was causing the inner turmoil in me to hit new heights. Without meaning to, I inched closer to him and had a strong desire to reach out and run my fingers through his dark blonde hair. Instead, I internally gave myself a hard smack, putting all parts of me in place, and focused back on the conversation.

"It's really aggravating you to be here, isn't it? Why me?" I asked, avoiding his request, because even if I wanted to, I couldn't actually help. I might be powerful, but I didn't mess with spells. That wasn't my specialty, and there was a difference between witch and fae magic. But before I told him that, I needed to know why he'd sought me out and who had told him how to find me.

His fingers pinched the bridge of his nose. "I know who you are. I know what you do. I've seen you in action before. I just need you to stop the king from killing my sister."

His words gave me pause. The king? As in King

Zephyr? No way in hell. I'd been done with Fae Islands for a long time, and I refused to go back. I didn't care if it was my only weakness. I'd moved on from my past... or so I told myself frequently.

"I'm sorry, but I can't help you. You need a witch for undoing a spell. Good luck." Uncaring about needing answers any longer, I turned to walk away before I did something stupid, like try to fight him until we ended up at my apartment to really take some aggressions out. Instead of letting me walk away, he grabbed on to my left arm, forcing me back to him.

Our bodies collided, and I sucked in a breath at the feel of his hard lines pressing against me. My skin shivered as my heartbeat sped up, a reaction I certainly wasn't prepared for. Gods, I really needed to let off some steam, but even *I* knew doing so with a fae wasn't the best idea.

I arched a brow at him, telling myself that I needed to kick his ass and move on, but I couldn't force my actions to match my thoughts for some reason. "Remove your hand or I'll show you why I was kicked out of Fae Islands in the first place."

He didn't move. In fact, his head inched closer, and beneath the ire he was emitting, I relished in the fact he was battling something within as well.

"I'm not leaving without your agreement to help." His voice was still strained.

"Why is this so hard for you?" I asked—again, ignoring his pleading—and focused on the tension set in his wide shoulders and the creases around his eyes.

"Because you are everything I hate about our world,

but I'm desperate and hoping you're not the monster you used to be. So, here I am, at your mercy, begging for help, because I'm not enough to free my sister from the mess she's gotten herself into. Now, will you come with me to Fae Islands, or are you still the heartless punisher I remember?"

CHAPTER 4

Fae Islands. The one place I had sworn I'd never return to. A harsh rejection sat at the edge of my tongue, but this unknown fae was piquing my curiosity for some reason. I wasn't ready to dismiss him just yet.

Get away from him. If you won't kill him, then move on before he ruins you.

My inner voice was taking on too many opinions. Maybe I was more off than I was even aware of. Clearly, none of my earlier pondering had done me any good.

"What's your name?" I asked while taking a step back. I needed my wits about me to concentrate if his problem concerned my old home. I wouldn't be weak enough to allow sexual tension or whatever was going on inside me to be a distraction.

"Finn Barlow, from North Island."

Ahh, his contempt for me made more sense. I recalled one particular time when I'd drawn quite the crowd on North Island. It was shortly after King

Zephyr had destroyed my doll and I'd needed to show him I was worthy of his love, or so he'd said.

"There are farmers on that island who think they know how to run these lands better than I do, but they will only destroy our paradise. Show them we're stronger, Lucinda. Bring fear into their hearts. Can you do that for me? Can you make me proud this time?"

"I won't disappoint you, my king. I'll be whatever you need me to be in order to keep our home safe."

I'd gone to North Island and burned two crop fields and an orchard that day. I'd killed more than a dozen fae and put that fear right where the king had wanted. He'd even rewarded me with a new doll after that, but I'd never even touched it after sticking it in the back of my closet.

"Well, Finn Barlow of North Island. We have a bit of a problem."

He narrowed his silver eyes at me. "And what would that be?"

"Well, besides the fact that I can't remove spells like I've already said, I have no plans of returning to Fae Islands. Not a single one of them, so while I'd normally tell you I don't back down from a challenge, I can't do that with this one."

His next words made me laugh out loud. "I'll pay you."

"Honey, there isn't anything in this world you could pay me with that I can't obtain on my own."

"What about the king's head?"

His question made my heart stutter. Breathing became harder, and my wings tightened around me.

Clearly, I wasn't as over my past traumas as I would have liked, but I pushed those feelings aside and laughed once more. "The king is untouchable, and not worth my time."

He grinned, and it was the first time since he'd moved out of the shadows that he seemed comfortable. "A lot has changed since you left. The king is no longer the beloved leader everyone once thought him to be. His death would be celebrated across the islands if someone was capable of doing so."

"Even the West?" West Island was where King Zephyr lived, and he allowed only the richest, strongest, most useful, and most loyal to stay within close proximity of his castle.

"Even there."

A flicker of emotion I hadn't felt in years sparked within me, but while I was reckless most of the time, I wasn't stupid.

The purr of Black Widow entered the alleyway, and I was saved from responding. Neva parked under the light, and I took in her ashen face. She was scared to death of handling my pride and joy.

I waved her over as she inched out of the car with the utmost care and tossed the keys at me as if nothing made her happier than to no longer be responsible for my baby.

Neva joined me at my side but said nothing while appraising the fae before us.

Finn stepped forward, held out his hand, and introduced himself. "I'm Finn."

Neva opened her mouth to reply, but as their hands

touched, she jerked hers away before he could hold on for too long. His face creased as she moved to stand a little further behind me.

Now that Neva was back, I realized I'd let my curiosity stop me from taking what I needed from the fae: a release of my dark magic.

I'd been allowing myself to get distracted too often lately, further proving it was time for a change. I couldn't become complacent. Not ever again.

"So, are you going to help my sister or not?" Finn asked as awkward silence settled around us.

My arms rose, and I tucked my wings away while faking a yawn. I was done dealing with him and the memories that he'd roused within me. "It's late and I've had a long day. How about you stalk me tomorrow and I'll let you know then? Say, around lunchtime?"

"How do I know you won't disappear?" he challenged.

"If you know so much about me, then you should also be aware that I never run from anything. This town is my home, and I won't let another fae run me out of it. Now, piss off and come back tomorrow or don't. I don't really care. You've made me cranky, and I want sleep."

He rolled his eyes before spreading wings that were leather and a green so deep, it was almost black in the dim light. I was only slightly disappointed they weren't gossamer like I'd pictured earlier.

Without another word, he wrapped his wings around himself and disappeared.

I turned to Neva, who was trembling. "What's wrong?"

"He is full of darkness, Lucy. You need to be careful."

For the first time ever, she'd called me Lucy, but I didn't dwell on that milestone. Instead, I was left wondering how the hell she'd read the darkness in him when I'd somehow missed it.

It was time to head out of town and let my darker side free. I was too distracted and needed to be fully present before Finn showed up again. Otherwise, I just might do something I'd regret.

AFTER DROPPING NEVA AT THE APARTMENT, I'D TAKEN OFF on my own, racing Black Widow through the traffic that never seemed to stop in LA, even at two in the morning. Once I was out of town and alone, only then did I scream my frustrations and let go of my hold on the dark magic threatening to consume me.

I ended up spending nearly two hours out in the wild, letting my power take charge and decimating half a forest in the process. I knew it was wrong to take my lack of control out on the earth, but it was either that or the humans.

When I was as satisfied as I was going to get, I'd made my way back home in hopes of sleeping, but for the rest of the early morning, I was assaulted by dreams —well, more like nightmares—of my old home every time I closed my eyes.

Memories broke through of my first days in the palace and believing when King Zephyr had promised to treat me like the daughter he'd never been able to have, to make me a princess. For the first year until I'd hit full maturity, he'd been the nicest fae I'd ever known. All of the mental conditioning I'd been through back then made me shudder now that I knew better.

Then, on my tenth birthday, he'd thrown me the largest party with more gifts than I had ever imagined, inviting every member of his guard. I'd never felt more special until the night ended and he'd come to my room with a gleam in his eyes I'd never seen before.

"It's time for you to repay me, Lucinda. Tomorrow, you'll begin putting those lovely wings of yours to use by training with the other guards and I want no complaints. Just remember how much I've done for you. You don't want to disappoint me, do you?"

The feel of his fingers grasping my chin seemed so real as I shook the memory off, letting wrath rise to the surface instead.

I'd been so naïve. So afraid that if I didn't do everything he asked, I'd once again be tossed out like the previous day's trash. He'd known my fears and planned it all perfectly. He'd made me believe I needed the only thing I'd craved as a child—a family. He'd pretended to be my family, but none of it had been real.

And now, he was going to die by the monster he'd created.

Well, only if I decided to help Finn.

While my time under the king's thumb hadn't been the highlight of my life, it had taught me enough to know I couldn't make emotional decisions. Finn's favor had stirred up too much of my past, and I wouldn't rush into making my final choice.

After deciding there would be no real rest for me, I trudged down the hallway away from my bedroom to the kitchen where Neva was already waiting with coffee in hand.

I accepted the cup and took a sip, but the taste didn't satisfy me like normal. "Do we have anything on the agenda today?" I asked her, hoping there would be something to distract me from my thoughts.

She shook her head. "Beatrix is the only one who has reached out lately. Seems the streets of LA are relatively quiet in the peak of winter."

Of course, they were. Almost as if it was perfect timing for Finn to show up and ask for my help.

"What are you going to do about the fae?" Neva asked, as if she knew exactly where my thoughts had gone.

"I don't know. I swore I'd never go back, but all I could think about last night was the chance to cut the king down. He's been a bastard ever since his sister died, but I hadn't seen it until it was too late. He doesn't deserve to rule those lands."

Usually, when someone didn't deserve something—and I knew it—I took it from them. At least, that was who I'd been the last couple years since I'd been banished, but I still remembered that final day like it was yesterday.

Standing guard outside the castle doors, I was staring up at the moon when Carden came snarling from the back side of the building. He was King Zephyr's pet werewolf. Some poor shifter who made a deal with the king and lost. It wasn't natural to keep a man in his beast form for long periods of time, but the king was insistent he had things under control.

"What's wrong, Carden?" I asked, holding my stance even as he began foaming at the mouth. Though the wolf couldn't respond with words, I hoped he'd show whatever had his tail ruffled.

Instead, his reply was a vicious growl right before he lunged at me with teeth bared. I was slammed with dark magic but managed to push him off me with my wings. Before I could grab on to the beast, he was headed inside the castle.

I yelled for help, but nobody responded. It was the middle of the night, and anyone who was on guard stood outside. Problems directly in the castle weren't usually something we had to worry about. Realizing I was on my own, I gave chase and flew over the stairs to catch up with Carden.

I landed in front of him as he clawed at the floor. "What do you think you're doing?" Magic poured off me in waves. I didn't want to kill the shifter. Something was clearly wrong with him, but he seemed to be headed directly to King Zephyr's chambers and I wouldn't let that happen. No matter what.

But even as I thought the words, Carden had other ideas. He howled loudly and charged for me, but I was ready this time. With my feathered wings turned into weapons, I angled them in front of me and sliced at the wolf. Blood was seeping from his chest, but that didn't hinder his attack.

He chomped down on my wing, barely making a scratch, but enough to distract me as Carden jumped over me and continued down the hallway. I wasn't going to be able to stop *the wolf without killing him. King Zephyr would be pissed, but at least he'd be alive.*

Shaking the memory from my head, I did my best not to remember what happened next. I hated more than anything that the king's betrayal still affected me, but it had also given me the freedom I hadn't known I needed at the time.

It wasn't all bad, but lately, I was having a hard time figuring out who I was, which made the decision of whether or not to help Finn even harder. If I let the past bring doubts into my mind, I wouldn't be able to stop the king.

Neva stared at me expectantly but didn't say a word. I knew what she was thinking, though I wasn't ready to accept it and probably never would be.

King Easton Zephyr was my kryptonite. He'd been like a father to me, and when he'd cast me out, it had changed me.

That was the day I'd promised to never be vulnerable again. That day, I'd become the hardened, uncaring fae I was now.

Apparently, my badass persona only extended as far as the bubble I'd created for myself in LA, but I refused to show a single weakness to anyone else. This would pass, and I could go back to enjoying my life and forgetting about Fae Islands.

But then there was the little incessant voice in my head reminding me that I hadn't really been enjoying anything as of late. I'd been out of sorts and uncertain what to do about it. I hated to believe this was my solution, that revisiting my past might be the only way for me to move forward once again.

But I'd worked too hard to go backward, or so I kept telling myself.

Don't wait for Finn. Killing the king will set you free from the pain you've been wallowing in. Do this and live the life you've always wanted. My inner voice was calmer than it had been in days. It was almost soothing, which made me trust it even less. It was reminding me too much of the king.

"You're a good person, Ms. Lucinda. You help those who need it whenever you can. If you're not able to this time, then there's nothing wrong with that. Whatever you decide will be the right choice. I'm sure the sister will be fine," Neva added minutes after our conversation had ended.

I'd tried not to think about the sister Finn had mentioned. I didn't want to be guilted into anything, but apparently, Neva wasn't above that kind of low blow.

I was then wondering what the king might have done to the girl that had driven her brother to come all this way to find me when it was obviously so hard for him to do.

I groaned as I imagined all the things I knew the bastard was capable of, and the sliver of compassion I still had left in me—the parts I'd been unable to let go of no matter how many times King Zephyr beat me into submission—rose to the surface.

"Son of a bitch," I muttered.

Neva smirked, trying to hide her happiness, but failing. "Shall I begin packing?"

"Not yet. Tell me about this darkness you sensed in Finn. What had you backing away from him?"

She carefully poured herself a cup of coffee before meeting my eyes. "Well, he reminded me of you… but a forced version."

I leaned back in the stool, staying calm. "Care to expand on that?"

"You were born a dark fae. Even though every fae has a dark ancestor in their bloodline, some of them are called light fae. Do you know why that is?"

I sighed. "Of course, I do." Every fae learned as a young faeling that the supernatural world depended on a balance. Where there was darkness, there would always be light, and vice versa, but no one person could be equally both.

I was born a dark fae. I would always be the darkness, no matter how many others I helped. There was no true redemption for someone like me.

"Well, Finn isn't a dark fae. He's a light one, but he's taken on enough dark magic that he should be dead. Yet, somehow, he's not. Last night, that fact scared me, but after spending so much time with you, I decided not to be frightened. Now, I'm curious like I think you are as well."

That damn elf was too observant.

"That is certainly interesting. So, are you saying you think we should help him even though it could get us killed?" I asked, because she needed to know if we stepped beyond the borders of Fae Islands, there was no going back. I wouldn't leave until either myself or the king was dead.

"May I be frank?" She paused, and I nodded because I wasn't the only one who had changed. She deserved a voice. "I think you've waited long enough to find your way home. While you might adore LA, you'll never truly be happy until you've buried your demons, Ms. Lucinda."

Damn it all to hell. Why did her thoughts have to mimic mine so closely?

A dark laugh escaped from me. "I have been saying I needed a bigger challenge. I don't think we can get much bigger than this."

Killing King Zephyr wouldn't be easy, but I'd grown in the three years since I was banished. He'd taught me how to be ruthless, but I'd grown to be smarter than he could ever dream of. Now, his choices were going to come back to take a damn chunk out of his ass.

A renewed sense of strength filled me. I wouldn't be weak to the fear he elicited from me.

I was better than him, and I needed to remember that.

"Shall I find Mr. Finn?" Neva asked.

I smirked. "No. Let him find us. One thing you need to remember: a woman should never chase a man. It gives him the advantage, and that leaves her vulnerable, and in this house, that's one thing we don't do."

She nodded, still standing before me, waiting for what to do next.

"Let's pack, but not everything." I glanced around

the room. "This is still home. We'll be back after we've killed the king."

Neva seemed disappointed by my answer, but I brushed it off. Even if Fae Islands was no longer ruled by a psychopath, I had no intentions of staying when the task was done. There were too many shitty memories.

LA was exactly where I was meant to be, and it was what I'd keep repeating, even as something unknown swirled inside me trying to convince me otherwise.

CHAPTER 5

Finn arrived exactly at noon. He was on my balcony staring through the glass while I enjoyed my lunch inside. I pretended not to notice him while I finished my salad and read the paper. I couldn't help but enjoy the fact that the longer I refused to look up, the more it seemed to infuriate him. Based upon the increased pacing I could see out of the corner of my eye, he was livid.

I stole glances, taking him in under the light unlike I'd been able to the night before. His broad shoulders and dark blonde hair were just as sexy as they'd been in the alley, but it was his wings I was really able to appreciate from the table.

The deep olive leather was free of any blemishes and held together by thick veins. I'd thought he was a warrior, but the lack of scars made me second-guess that notion. If he wasn't, it was a waste. He'd clearly been built for battle with his towering height and layers of muscle.

Nearly ten minutes after he'd arrived, his wingtips tapped on the glass, and I was impressed with his patience. Instead of rewarding him, I held my finger up, finishing the page I wasn't actually reading before popping one last piece of tomato into my mouth. After I set the newspaper down, I folded my napkin and brushed it over my lips as I met his silver eyes and moaned. "Damn, that's good food. Would you like some?"

There might have been a glass door between us, but I knew he could hear me. His head shook twice as he glowered.

"Neva, dear, can you let our guest in?" I called and put my attention back on the paper I normally only read for entertainment. The things humans fought over were ridiculous and pathetic. Sad, even. Maybe one day, the supernatural race would take over and show them a thing or two.

I chuckled at the thought. Like our leaders would ever let that happen.

Neva appeared and unlocked the balcony door, letting Finn in. He offered her a kind smile before returning his snarl to me, which further amused me. Mostly because I was the one he needed help from, yet he was furious with me. Instead of being irritated with his surliness, I focused on the fact his eyes hadn't strayed far from mine.

"Have you made your choice yet?" he deadpanned.

My right finger tapped against my cheek as I remained seated even though he towered over me. I didn't need him thinking he frightened me. "I'm not sure. How about you tell me more about your sister and the trouble she's found herself in with King Zephyr?"

A twitch appeared in his cheek, and I liked that the longer I held his stare, the more pronounced the twinge became. Even more so, I enjoyed that he didn't seem to be at all afraid of me like most fae were.

As we had our stare-down, I took in the finer details I hadn't been able to see during previous stolen glances. His eyes weren't only silver, but also a darker charcoal color around the iris that would have been easy to miss for someone not paying close attention. Good for me, I was always paying attention.

His hair was short all around and dark blonde, while his skin was just a few shades lighter. His sharp jaw caught my attention next, along with defined lips that were probably full and lush on a normal day but were currently thinned while I took my time drinking him in with abandon.

"Are you done?" he snapped.

"Well, if you want to spin in a circle, I'll happily continue, but if you'd rather get straight to business, then take a seat."

He mumbled something about this being a horrible idea but sat anyway. Before he could say anything else, I was ready with questions I'd already prepared. Even though I had decided to help his sister, I wouldn't do it blindly.

"Why do you contain dark magic when you're a light fae?" I asked first and his mouth popped open, but there was no reply, so I continued. "You came to me for a reason. Don't be so shocked I noticed." Okay, that was a lie, but he didn't need to know it was Neva who'd pointed out the darkness.

Finn grimaced and leaned back in the chair, allowing his long legs to extend beneath the glass tabletop. I didn't miss the chance to watch his dark-wash jeans tighten around the muscles of his thighs.

"Like I said before, my sister is in trouble. I tried to fix it myself, and it didn't work out. The dark magic is my consequence to deal with and not why I'm here. So, why don't we keep the conversation around her and the piece-of-shit king who hurt her?" At the mention of the king, the charcoal in his eyes bled through the silver, and I sensed his ire rising in the air around us.

Good. Finn would need that rage to accomplish what he hoped.

"So, then. What happened to this sister of yours? What can she do that the king couldn't resist meddling with?" I asked, letting the previous question go without a real answer. I'd get it out of him when he wasn't paying close enough attention.

"My sister is a healer, but not the normal kind that can only heal wounds. Ivy can take sickness away as well." As he spoke about his sister, his face softened and the lush lips I knew existed came into view. "The king was sick and demanded Ivy heal him when his own personal healer failed to do so herself."

I shrugged, not understanding what the big deal was. "If Ivy's a healer, what's the problem? Isn't that what she's supposed to do?"

Healers were only ever born from light fae parents. I assumed this was a choice by the gods that created us.

A light fae would have the least chance of becoming selfish with their abilities and more likely to use their gifts for the greater good. Dark fae had a little more rebellion on the inside, but that was what made us great warriors.

"When Ivy heals a sickness from someone, she doesn't just make it go away. She takes on the illness herself. Normally, her body is able to fight it off better and faster than a normal fae, so long as the disease isn't deadly." His jaw tightened as his eyes darkened. Compassion flickered inside me, but I stuffed it down before it could grow. This was an assignment. I couldn't get emotionally involved, no matter how badly my fingers itched to slide under the table and calm his bouncing thigh.

"The king was supposed to die, but your sister saved him and now *she's* dying," I summarized, focusing on the task and confident I'd read between the lines correctly, even though he seemed to struggle with precise words.

"Not exactly. That is what was supposed to happen, but the king promised her she'd live."

Ah, fae royalty couldn't outright lie to their people. It was something spelled into the crowning ceremony long ago to protect the people, but there were always ways around the old law.

Finn continued, "The only question Ivy ever asks is if the illness is deadly, and instead of the king telling her yes or no, he'd merely said she'd live. What he actually meant was he'd have a witch cast a spell on her that keeps her body frozen as if she was a vampire.

"Ivy won't ever get the chance to age up or have kids or anything she should be allowed until the king is killed and the poison within her body is removed. And the witch linked the spell to the king's lifeline, so we end him, we end the spell. I've done what I can for her, but she's now refusing my help, which is where you come in."

Fae aged in three stages once they reached maturity at ten and were no longer considered a faeling. We had our "prime" that lasted about five decades, during which we'd appear somewhere between the ages of eighteen and twenty-one human years.

"Midlife" was next, which was when most people settled down and were ready to have a family, depending on their fae role. We continued to age during that time period until we appeared about forty.

The last aging stage was the "after years". Fae go through their last aging cycle and, if they'd lived that long, could appear somewhere in their fifties or sixties for several centuries. It was something to be celebrated to make it to the after years, though not anything I'd ever seen for myself when I worked for the king.

"So, let me make sure I understand this correctly. You tried to save your sister but ended up taking on dark magic while practicing with power you had no business dabbling in." When the twitch returned, I grinned, knowing I'd figured it out on my own. "In the process of all that, she got pissed at you and now you're desperate for me to help before she does something stupid."

He opened his mouth to object, but I held my finger up and, surprisingly, he complied, staying silent.

"Now, I'm supposed to be some saving grace that figures out not only how to kill the king, so the spell dies along with him, but how to get the death poison out of her as well, once she's no longer protected by the witch's magic. Did I catch all of that right?"

His teeth ground together as he nodded stiffly.

Unfortunately, I had no clue how to remove the poison she'd taken from the king. There were very few things in this world that could kill fae royalty without the use of specialized weapons. The first thing I'd need to do was meet his sister and see for myself what was going on with her.

"I can't promise to save your sister, but if the king's death is consolation enough, I can promise to kill him," I said with a conviction I hadn't been sure of until that moment.

"You can't kill him until we save her," Finn raged.

I inched forward, leaning across the glass, and caught his eyes darting down to my chest for the briefest of seconds. At least I knew the attraction I was experiencing wasn't completely one-sided, but I stayed on task.

"Well, I can't go back to Fae Islands and walk away without consequence if I *don't* kill him. So, you'll have to decide if the risk is worth it. I'm not saying I won't help try to save your sister, but at the end of the day, if we can't do that, King Zephyr will still die."

He considered my words before responding, and I let him have his time. I was in no hurry to venture back to Fae Islands. I was already letting plans formulate in my mind and wanted to sort them out fully before I acted.

Neva returned then, and I stood from the table to join her in the living room while Finn figured out how he wanted to proceed.

Sure, now that I'd accepted that I needed to bury my demons, I was set on returning regardless of his decision, but if he declined my help after our conversation, I'd at least give him some time to sort out his sister's issue before I began my hunt for the king.

I might be wicked, but I wasn't heartless.

I nudged Neva. "He's sort of a delicate flower. He needs a moment to decide if he really wants my help now that he knows what could happen."

A soft smile played at her lips. "I doubt there is *anything* delicate about that man."

I laughed at her forwardness. "Well, there is something broken about him at least." Finn carried a darkness in him I might not have seen the night before, but I couldn't ignore it now. A part of me wanted to break him completely until he was writhing beneath me and begging for more of whatever I was offering.

The thoughts took me by surprise. Even though I was no Mary Sue, I normally didn't like to mix business with pleasure. Though, the peculiarity of him made me want to toe the line and see what could happen.

I watched him from across the room as he steadied his breathing and stared out the window. If it wasn't for the tense set of his shoulders or the continuous tic in his jaw, I'd have assumed he was enjoying the view, but I knew that wasn't the case.

I might not have known what it was like to have a family of my own to care about, but I could see how hard of a choice he had before him.

Minutes later, Neva was once again gone and I was lounging on the couch when Finn stood above me. He was possibly wearing the same white shirt from the night before, or he really didn't like diversity. Either way, I enjoyed the view from my position and took in the slight ripple of muscles across his chest as he folded his arms.

"I'd like to let my sister choose, but she can't leave the islands. Is there a way we can compromise, and you can leave straight away if she says no?" With the strain back in his voice, I could tell it was maddening for him to be at my mercy.

I remembered the cloaking spell I'd asked Beatrix for. I'd originally gotten it in case the fae before me had proved to be a bigger problem than I'd been in the mood to handle, but the spell's usefulness would also work on Fae Islands. Just because I was curious what could possibly poison the king to the point of death, I agreed. "Under one stipulation. She only has an hour to decide. I won't wait around for days."

"Fine." His knuckles turned white from balling his hands so tightly and made his forearms bulge, but I ignored that fact and met his silver eyes that heated with a fiery passion the longer they stayed locked with mine.

My chest heaved, and his gaze ventured back to my

chest before returning to my face. He, too, had begun to breathe harder as tension built. There was something about him that called to me and made me curious, but I had years of practice in building my self-control.

"We leave first thing tomorrow. Be here before sunrise," I said aggressively, hoping to ease whatever was happening between us.

He nodded, then spread his wings before storming outside to disappear.

The thought of ending King Easton Zephyr should have been at the forefront of my thoughts, but instead, anytime I closed my eyes, Finn was the only thing that I could focus on.

He isn't good for us. You need to tell him no. The voice was back, but I still wasn't listening to it.

Finn was a temptation I would decide on my own if I wanted to ignore or not. Until then, I would keep my guard up and focus on what was being asked of me. This assignment was no different than any of the others. There was a bully and an innocent.

If I could keep my attention on the facts, then I could succeed without distraction and make this my most interesting assignment yet.

CHAPTER 6

ae Islands consisted of four primary isles and some smaller ones that were typically only used by other supernatural races for vacation. I'd lived on West Island during my fifteen years there, but I'd visited the East, North, and South ones to do the king's bidding on many occasions. Each one had its purpose and ran fine without King Zephyr, but he asserted himself whenever he felt like it. Or, at least, that was how it had been when I was there.

Finn said he was from North Island, and I'd have to watch my back there. Three years wasn't a long time for fae—more like a blink of the eye. My last task there for the king had been to punish a group of farmers for failing to pay their food tax.

Disgust rolled through me at the memory of my former self. Even though I still didn't often do things without selfish reason, my understanding of right and wrong had changed after spending time in LA on my own. Those fae hadn't deserved what I'd done to them.

"Are you ready, Ms. Lucinda?" Neva asked, stepping onto the balcony. She caught me gazing at the sky that was just beginning to change colors for the morning, filled with pinks and blues painted across the cloudless sky.

"Lucy. Please call me Lucy," I requested as I turned toward her and pushed my past behind me where it belonged.

She smiled softly. "I'll do my best."

"And yes, I'm ready. We're just waiting on—"

"I'm here." Finn landed on the balcony as if he owned the place, and my chest tightened as he walked through the open glass door.

His wings spread once more as he entered my home. Now that he'd shown them, he didn't seem to like to tuck them away. He'd also changed from a white shirt and dark jeans to a black tee and tan cargo pants with boots that matched his shirt and laced up to mid-shin.

He was appraising me just as openly as I had him, and I wondered what he saw when he looked at me. Did he see the me I let everyone else see, or were his silver eyes really as formidable as they appeared?

I was wearing black leather pants and another corset, but this one wasn't for fun; it was for combat and keeping all of my goods tucked in unless we needed them later.

My hair was braided to the side, and I flicked it back before bringing a hand to my hip. "You're very punctual, aren't you?"

"No, I just like to spend the least amount of time

with you as possible, so I don't show until I'm required. Otherwise, I'd be early."

His attitude didn't insult me. In fact, it did the opposite. Finn could act irritated all he wanted, but his reactions to me had been real. He was just pissed off that he was attracted to someone he thought was a monster. I didn't blame him for thinking that way since he'd only known me as the king's guard, and I wasn't entirely sure I was willing to show him I wasn't still that person.

Finn was hot, and his brooding attitude certainly drew me in, but those two things were also reasons to keep my space. There was something about him that could be a distraction, one I couldn't afford to allow in. Not when I was going to kill King Zephyr.

He greeted Neva with a kindness he'd yet to show me. "Good morning. Do you need help with anything?"

Her gaze darted back to me and then the fae again. "Um, no, Mr. Finn. I have everything taken care of for our trip."

"Please, call me Finn."

I laughed at his request, the same habit I'd been trying to break her of for much too long. "Good luck with that. Her manners are too ingrained to go without the formalities."

He sneered at me. "Well, maybe if you didn't treat her like a servant, she wouldn't feel the need to act like one."

"First off, screw you. I'm tired of your attitude toward me when you're the one who needs *my* help. Second, I don't force her to stay. She chooses to." My foot tapped, and it took everything in me not to flick a nasty blast of magic at him. Only my curiosity in finding out what had made the king vulnerable kept me in check.

"Right. I'm sure she *chooses* to be at your beck and call all day, every day."

He'd managed to turn the tables and rile me up like no supernatural before him. Gods, I'd known him for a day. Why in the world was I letting his disapproval of my life bother me? A small part of me was intrigued, but every other part was beyond frustrated and itching to lash out at him for being such an ass.

He mumbled something I couldn't hear and smirked as if he'd won. Aggravated beyond belief, I threw my hands in the air, accidentally letting magic flow from my fingers, and scorched my ceiling. Gods, I hadn't done that since I was eleven.

"Damn it, look what you made me do. Neva is not my servant. I'm not sure what you want me to do to show that. Give her a damn sock and say 'be free'?"

Neva stepped cautiously toward me. "It's okay, Lucy. I want to be here, and I promise to let you know when or if that changes."

The fact that she called me Lucy was the only thing that confirmed she was being honest. "Thank you, Neva."

Finn watched the interaction in silence and thankfully kept his mouth shut while I got control over my magic again. My chest heaved as I took deep breaths. I would not let this brooding fae get to me. I was better than my hormones.

That's right, Lucinda. Forget this fae and go out on your own. Kill the king and take the throne. Make them all bow to you, my inner voice added.

I don't want the throne. Never have, never will, I thought. There was no reply and I was thankful.

Neva reached for my arm before I could. "I think we should be going. His sister is waiting."

Her honey eyes pleaded with me to do the right thing, and another battle began within myself. Between the psycho voice in my head, Finn's attitude, and Neva's expectations of me, I was about to lose my shit. I only wanted to unleash my darkness on those who deserved it. The fact that I was reacting to Finn so strongly was keeping me on edge and erratic, two things that didn't bode well when heading into a mission. I needed to fix something.

I waltzed toward Finn, slammed my palm into his chest, and zapped him. "You are done talking to me like I'm beneath you. If you want my help, quit acting like an asshole only to me and show me some damn respect."

We were nearly nose-to-nose as he bent closer to me, and I heard the intake of Finn's breath once I was in his personal space. He tried to cover his reaction to my closeness with a smirk, but I hadn't missed how I'd affected him.

"I'll show you respect when you deserve it," he said with little emotion in his voice.

The heat from his chest coursed through my palm and up my arm, making me realize I was still touching him. *Damn him!* I pushed the towering fae away, annoyed even more when he didn't stumble. "Let's go."

Neva was already waiting at the balcony door, ready to lock up. I moved to stand under the awning and spread my wings, all the while doing my best to ignore Finn. I refused to look at him, worried too many of my feelings would be on display. I didn't want him to feel like he had any control over me.

Once Finn was out of my house and the door was locked, I grabbed on to Neva and disappeared without saying a word. If Finn was smart, he'd know to follow my trail before it dissipated. Teleporting always left a magical signature behind, but it only lasted a split second. If he wasn't quick enough, then my plans were about to change, and maybe I'd begin listening to the inner darkness that didn't ever want to shut the hell up.

In an instant, we went from downtown Los Angeles to Sri Lanka, an island at the tip of India. Neva and I were standing on a deserted beach, and I grinned. "I guess he isn't as smart as he is good looking."

Neva's eyes widened as she stared behind me.

"You're right. I'm smarter," he murmured in my ear as he passed by me, continuing toward the ocean.

Pissed at the way my skin reacted to his closeness, I flipped him off even though he couldn't see it. Neva shook her head at me. "Should you use the spell now, Ms. Lucinda?"

"I think that would be best." Bending down, I pulled the vial from my boot and swirled it around. "Hopefully Beatrix is as good as she says she is, or his sister won't get the hour I've promised."

Neva didn't seem worried as I pulled the cork on the glass bottle. The liquid smelled like lavender and citrus as I brought the sparkling contents to my lips and drank it in one gulp.

My wings unfurled, and the tips hardened on their own, narrowly missing Neva. She squeaked and backed up as my body glowed purple, then my normal teal. Power rushed through me, and I managed to point my hands downward just in time for magic to pour out of them and into the sand around us.

Finn was back and picked up Neva right before she could get zapped. Instead, he absorbed the power aimed for her. I tried to shut it off, but I couldn't, and I was ready to go back to LA and rip Beatrix's head clean off.

Another minute passed before I finally had control of my body again. "I'm going to kill her."

Finn stepped closer after he set Neva back down. "Actually, you should be thanking her. If I didn't know better, I'd think you were human."

It was the first time he'd spoken to me without some sort of attitude, but I was more shocked that he couldn't get a read on my magic, not even in the slightest. I assumed the witch's spell would only mask my particular magical signature, but based on Finn's words, it seemed as if she'd hidden my essence completely.

I closed my eyes and focused inward. My magic still swirled within me, and my wings were still present, which saved me from finding and killing Beatrix.

"Can you fly?" Finn asked.

I flapped my wings, and my feet lifted off the ground several inches. "Apparently so."

I reached for Neva, but Finn stepped between us. "How about I take Neva? If your body starts to reject the spell, you could hurt her."

A refusal sat at the tip of my tongue, but I swallowed it down. He was right, and I wouldn't risk my friend, because that was what she was to me, regardless of how much she also assisted me. "Fine, but only if she's okay with it."

Neva met my stare before answering. She'd been fearful of the darkness Finn contained before, so I wouldn't subject her to more if she still wasn't comfortable with it.

She finally nodded, then took a step closer to him. "I'll be fine."

"Well, now that everything is sorted, let's get on with it. We have a long flight ahead of us," I said and stretched my wings out. It had been months since I'd used them for any considerable amount of time, and I was eager.

Sri Lanka was the closest we could get to the islands by using magic. From there, the only way into Fae Islands was by flight or boat. The latter was only an option if we didn't need to stay under the radar. Teleporting there was out because there was no set entrance to the realm, and we had to have a physical place in mind for us to use that particular perk—not just the middle of the ocean.

The trip would take about two hours, and, even though we hadn't left the beach yet, I was ready for it to be over. The longer I had to see Finn, the more conflicted I became. Not only with him but myself, for reasons I was hoping I could work out before we landed.

I couldn't let anything distract me from what we were about to do. I knew I'd only get one shot at killing King Zephyr and if I failed, it meant I was dead and that wasn't an option I was willing to accept.

WHEN FAE ISLANDS' BOUNDARY CAME INTO VIEW, I HAD A hard time breathing normally. A panic swirled inside me I hadn't experienced since I was a child, and I didn't like it one damn bit.

My arms crossed to hide my trembling hands as I took in the shimmer of the forcefield that would transport us from Earth to a realm only supernaturals were allowed to access. The shimmer wasn't visible to humans, and if a human was out in the ocean on their boat or flying over in this exact spot, they would pass through it without being transported.

When we reached the portal, Finn paused, waiting for me to make the first move. I held my hand over the forcefield and took a deep breath.

I could do this. The king didn't control me any longer. I was stronger than he could ever dream of being. I was not the same fae as when I left three years ago.

With those words, I pushed through the magic with my wings and was floating in the fae realm before I could blink. Finn and Neva were right behind me, but I paid them no attention as I searched for any signs my presence had triggered a warning to the wrong people.

We hovered in the sky for several minutes, and once I confirmed nobody was coming for us, I finally relaxed enough to take in the beauty of my surroundings. East Island caught my attention first with its jungle-like forest and vibrant foliage. LA had nothing close to that. The nature was the only thing I missed about these lands.

Then, I focused on North Island. Crops and orchards took up most of the land while houses occupied the rest. The fae who lived there were more service-oriented and provided nearly all of the food to the other islands. They grew fruits and vegetables and harvested grains. Any animals that lived there were for work or companionship, because none of the fae I knew ate meat.

We only consumed what the animals gave us, like milk and eggs. In my darkest days, I'd considered eating a steak once. The humans certainly knew how to make them smell tantalizing, but when it was set in front of me, I couldn't do it. That day had been the first in which I began to find myself again. Or at least, the new me.

Though, I wasn't sure that was true. I'd found the person I thought I was supposed to be, but arriving back here and being around Finn and Neva was showing me I still had a lot to learn.

The sky around us was clear and the air refreshing. For the first time in a long while, I could take a deep inhale and not taste exhaust. Though, none of the beauty or cleanliness took away from the fact I wasn't welcome on the islands.

With that reminder, I sped up, and Finn did, too. We needed to get out of sight as quickly as possible or his sister's decision wouldn't soon matter.

Finn dipped down low and flew into an orchard, so I followed. The trees grew oranges and apples, then further on I saw pomegranates, my favorite. I snagged one as we began to slow, and a house came into view. Finn landed first and set Neva down, who wobbled but caught herself, so I kept my interest on the fruit in my hand.

My nails dug into the hardened shell and broke it in half. Just as I picked out a clump of seeds with my fingers, a woman stormed out of the house several yards in front of us. "Who the hell do you think you are eating our food?"

CHAPTER 7

$\mathcal{I}$ ignored her and took my time enjoying the juicy seeds, while keeping one eye on the female who inched closer. She tucked her blonde hair behind her ear, then surprised me with a grin before leaping and wrapping her arms around me. The action caused me to drop the fruit, and I raised a brow at Finn while keeping my arms at my side.

"I was totally kidding. Eat all you want. Well, so long as you're Lucinda." She stepped back, but still held on to my arms. "I'm Ivy. Thank you for not finding my brother as repulsive as I do and actually listening to him. I really thought you wouldn't come, and then we'd be in even more trouble, because he probably would have pissed you off. Then, on top of the king, I would have had to worry about you coming after us, and damn, this whole thing is a lot to take in."

Holy shit. Who the hell was this girl, and why did she talk so damn fast?

Finn sighed. "Ivy, leave her alone. She's not our friend and certainly doesn't want your hugs."

She released me and whirled around to face him, blonde hair flying around her as she pointed a finger into his chest. "You shut your dirty mouth. I wasn't talking to you, and Lucinda didn't seem to mind." She turned back to me. "Right?" Her big doe eyes stared at me, and I cringed.

Gods, what was I doing here?

"I have no opinion on whatever it is you do. I'm just here to let you know what *I'm* willing to do, and if you're good with the risks, then I'll stay. If not, I'm out of here. For now."

My words caused her to frown, but I didn't let it get to me. I had to get my walls back up and stop letting feeble emotions rule my decisions. I wasn't there to be friends with these people. I'd only come to figure out what kind of sickness she had and use that knowledge to destroy the king. If it helped them at the same time, then so be it.

Back in LA, I might have been all about helping the little guy against a tormenter, but I was quickly realizing that I could lose who I was to these people if I put them first. King Zephyr was no ordinary bully, and this would be unlike any assignment before.

Ivy circled me, then glanced at Neva and back at me. "Why can't I sense any magic from you even though you have wings, but she has no wings and I can feel her magic?"

I winked. "I'm special."

She snorted. "Right. Seriously, though. Why?"

Finn stepped closer and grabbed her elbow. "Ivy, that's enough."

She appraised me once more, and I was finding it hard to get a read on her. She had the snark I usually enjoyed, but there was a goodness about her that made me uncomfortable. I didn't often spend time with the people I helped. Especially not since Neva had begun helping me.

"You really think she can help us?" Ivy asked Finn, as if I wasn't standing right next to them.

"I do. She has her own motivations and actually, we need to talk about those, so let's get inside before anyone sees her. You might not remember Lucinda, but I know plenty of others who will."

Neva approached me as I ignored Finn's words and snagged another fruit since Ivy had knocked mine out of my hands with her lack of grace. Breaking it in half, I gave one side to Neva before digging into the other. I was hesitant to follow Finn and Ivy into their house, and Neva knew it. She was getting too good at reading me.

"How are you doing?" Neva asked between chews, and I sensed her eyes trying to see something in mine that I wouldn't allow her to find—fear.

"I've never been better. Let's get this over with." I finished the pomegranate half and tossed it behind me before we entered the small farmhouse.

Any emotions or worries I'd been letting get to me earlier were safely tucked away. I knew what needed to be done, and I wouldn't let foolish things like feelings— mine or anyone else's—distract me. Not even the way

Finn made my skin heat when he leveled his silver eyes on me.

Ignoring those thoughts, I moved past him as he waited at the door for us and gestured toward the left. The first thing I saw was a small living area with one wooden rocking chair and a tattered brown couch. Ivy came skipping into the room from behind the doorway and pushed her way past her brother before taking the chair.

She watched me intently, but I didn't mind. I did the same back to her. She was maybe an inch shorter than me. Her light green eyes stood out against her sun-kissed skin and held a pureness that I'd never known.

I opted to stand and leaned against the wall with my knee bent and arms crossed. My hope was the stance would keep Ivy from throwing herself at me again. I didn't do hugs. I'd have rather made out with Dante the bloodsucker.

Neva took a place on the couch, still eating her fruit, picking at the seeds with her nimble fingers, and Finn found a spot on the wall across from me. I arched my brow at him. "Would you like to do the honors, or shall I?"

He ignored me and turned his attention to his sister. "So, we have a bit of a problem."

Ivy crossed her legs and feigned surprise with a gasp. "You wouldn't say?"

His chest grumbled. "Now is not the time for your special brand of sarcasm, Ivy."

"But it's so much fun." She pouted and I decided I

could like her a little more, as long as she kept her hands to herself.

Neva sighed, likely pity for Finn because she understood exactly how he felt.

"Like I was saying, there's a problem. Lucinda is willing to kill the king, but she can't do anything about the spell or poison you took on. We can search for someone who can at the same time as finding a way to get to King Zephyr, but there are no guarantees we will. If Lucinda is able to kill him before we can prepare a witch, or another capable fae, then you could die." That last bit caused the color to leave Finn's face, as if the reality of losing his sister was finally hitting him.

"I didn't want to take this choice from you, but I need you to know that I can figure out another way. We don't have to take Lucinda's help," he added when Ivy didn't respond.

"Right, because letting you take on dark magic in hopes you'll figure out how to remove the spell yourself has been working so well. I won't live the rest of my life as a prisoner, Finn. I'm ready to be free, and if the only way that can happen is in death, then that's what it will be. King Zephyr doesn't deserve to live any longer." Her resolve was something to be admired, and if I'd met her before the king had broken my innocence, I could have seen us being friends.

She turned to me. "Do whatever you need to in order to end the king. Just make sure he can't do to anyone else what he's done to me ever again. I don't care about the consequences."

Finn moved toward his sister, bending down onto

his knees and taking her hand. "Ivy, I can't lose you, too. Please, think this through. Think of Maddox."

The ache in his voice pulled at me at the same time I wondered who Maddox was. The curiosity didn't outweigh the emotions and I wanted to stab someone. Why the hell was I allowing myself to care that he was hurting?

Because he makes you weak. You need to get—

I closed my eyes and pushed the voice away with a wave of my own power. I was getting really annoyed with it. I'd never had my subconscious be so loud, not even when I needed it most. This was how I really knew I was losing it and had to figure out a way to find myself again. Maybe revisiting my past wasn't the way to move forward.

I shook my head and pushed away from the wall. I needed space. Lots of it. "I'll be outside. Remember, I only promised to wait an hour and the clock started the moment we crossed the forcefield."

Without waiting for a reply, I headed back outside and slammed the door behind me. When I was twenty paces out, I heard the door open and shut behind me. Neva was likely coming after me, but I didn't want her to guilt me for my abrupt retreat, so I picked up my speed and spread my wings.

Then, I remembered I wasn't actually welcome on any of the islands and there was nowhere for me to go. Son of a bitch. What was I thinking coming back before I was actually prepared to kill the king?

Something about Finn Barlow was screwing with

me, and I needed to get the hell away from whatever was happening.

There was a warmth blossoming in my chest that made me physically sick from the overwhelmingness of it. At the same time, the dark shadow within my mind was getting louder.

While I didn't agree with the voice in my head, it was safe from hurt and betrayal. It would keep me from being vulnerable. It was exactly what I needed to hold on to. Wasn't it?

Kill them. Kill the king.

I shook my head. I couldn't kill them, but I would end the king. Ivy had already said she didn't care what happened to her. I'd be doing everyone a favor, but most importantly, myself. Yes, this was my path. No more feelings or distractions, just doing.

Decision made, I spread my wings and lifted my feet from the ground with one flap. I didn't even bother to glance back at Neva. She'd be fine with them. I couldn't afford to allow her the chance to change my mind. I'd come back for her later.

Just when I was maybe five feet in the air, rough hands grabbed my waist and jerked me back down. "I don't think so," Finn hissed as I smashed into his chest, knocking us both to the ground.

Damn him for being so tall. I landed on top of him, and my still-spread wings hardened and caged us in, barely missing his arms. My legs tangled in his, and our hips lined up almost perfectly, allowing me to file away just a few more details about him that I really didn't need.

With my wings supporting me, I stared down at him with no emotion. "And here, I thought you couldn't stand me."

His eyes heated, the charcoal melting through the lighter silver until there was none left. Based on the hardened twitch between us, I felt confident I was right and continued, a plan forming as I spoke.

I raised my hand and cupped his chin between my fingers. "You get even hotter when you're angry. Let's see what happens when I do this." I gave him one second to object before my lips pressed against his, and I took what I had no business wanting.

Finn kissed me back, and I knew it was time to go. He'd done the opposite of what I'd anticipated. Moving my hands south, I sent the tiniest shock of magic through his ribs to get the reaction I desired.

His hand grabbed on to my braid and yanked my head back. "Lucinda," he growled against my lips as I smirked.

"Yes, Finn?" I batted my lashes.

"That's enough."

That, I wouldn't argue with.

"I agree. We need some separation and don't feel too bad, but it's definitely you and not me." I inched my wings closer, supporting my body with my knees. Before he could move, I pooled magic into both hands and trapped him with a bit of extra power and feathers I didn't mind leaving behind if it meant I could get the hell away from him.

"What are you doing, Lucinda?" he snarled, bucking beneath my magic.

"Exactly what you expected of me."

Neva poked her head out the door, but I didn't acknowledge her. I couldn't let anything else stop me.

My wings extended to their full six-foot span, and I took to the sky, heading straight for King Easton Zephyr.

It didn't matter that I hadn't settled on a plan. All that mattered was that I was done letting him win.

CHAPTER 8

Nobody chased after me, and I should have been happy about that, but I wasn't even close to okay. Since I couldn't understand why the situation irritated me so badly, I focused on figuring out how best to get close to the king without him knowing.

While I sped away from their farm, I wasn't exactly watching where I was going, my thoughts too focused on how best to complete my task. I could attack head-on, take out whoever was in my way while moving through the castle like it was mine, but that was reckless. I didn't know what had changed in the last three years.

Then, there was the option of finding someone to glamor me. Between a glamor and the spell Beatrix had given, I could possibly walk right in, but again, I'd run the risk of being questioned if I tried to go anywhere the public wasn't normally allowed. One wrong answer could turn into a war within the castle where I'd be severely outnumbered.

Only one option was left, but it was one that wouldn't provide instant gratification and would require my stay on the islands to be much longer than I wanted, but this last option was definitely the one he wouldn't expect from me. Not from the Lucinda he thought I was.

By the time I began paying attention to where I was again, I was nearing West Island and considering turning toward South Island. After thinking it through more thoroughly, I knew I wasn't ready to initiate my plans. I had no weapon, and I still knew nothing about the poison that nearly killed King Zephyr. Though, I also wasn't ready to go back to Finn's farm.

I'd only been flying for about ten minutes and was surprised I hadn't seen anyone else. When I'd last been around, people flew between the lands frequently, but everything around me was quiet. Too quiet.

The islands here were bigger than any I'd seen while on Earth, and they weren't very far from each other, which was a good thing once I realized nothing was as it should be. I needed to get out of the open.

I headed for an orchard at the edge of South Island. My wings carried me down, and I landed without noise, heading straight for the cover of trees. I'd missed the nature of these lands and reached out for the closest limb, but as soon as my fingers connected with the branch, brittle leaves crumbled to the ground. "What the hell?"

Then, I started paying closer attention and took in a deep inhale of death.

The dirt beneath my feet that used to be powdered

and fresh was now hard and cracked. The trees I could see held no food or flowers, and when I pressed my hand against several trunks, there was no life left within any of them.

My feet moved of their own accord as I stared at what was left. Everything was dying, and I was taken aback by the emotions it caused within me.

Up ahead, a little boy darted out from behind a tree. He was maybe six or seven and covered in red grime. His bright blue eyes watched me, and I couldn't tell if they were filled with fear or curiosity.

I knew I should go. I told myself to just flap my wings and leave, but my extremities weren't listening. My feet continued forward until I reached the child.

"Hi," he squeaked with a wave of his hand.

I offered a tight smile back. Saving kids was one thing; interacting with them was something I'd never been comfortable with. "Hello. Where are your parents?"

He pointed up, and I hoped he meant they were just out flying.

"Are you alone right now?" I asked.

He shook his head. "You're here."

Clever boy. "What happened to the trees?"

He glanced around, then moved closer to me and whispered, "The king tried to kill them."

I kneeled down in front of him. "Why would he do that to his own home?"

"My teetee said it's because he's selfish, but I think he was just having a bad day."

"Did you see him when he was having a bad day?"

The boy nodded. "Did he hurt you?" It wasn't like I needed to add more fuel to my need for vengeance, but it couldn't be a bad thing, either.

"No, I hid in the trees and they protected me until he was done, then I ran home."

I patted his head awkwardly. "Why don't you run home now? It's not safe to be out here by yourself."

"Are you going to make the trees all better?" he asked, tears brimming in his soft blue eyes.

I sighed, knowing I should have just gone home. I damn well knew better. "I don't have the power to do that, unfortunately."

He frowned. "But the trees said you did, and the trees are never wrong."

Gossamer emerald wings sprouted from his shoulders, and he flew off before I could formulate a response. Once he was out of sight, I still didn't know what to think about the interaction or if I should just believe the direction my mind was taking me.

Fae that could communicate with nature were rare, even more uncommon than those with wings like mine. If he was being truthful, that boy needed to learn how to keep his abilities to himself or he'd soon find himself a pawn in something much bigger than his beloved trees.

I turned to leave, knowing I couldn't stay hidden on a dying land, not even with my power concealed. With my wings fully extended and ready for flight, I moved them once before a very angry fae dropped down in front of me.

"Why are you still here?" Finn challenged.

"Why are you following me?" I countered instead of answering.

He sighed, the irritation he'd shown just seconds before slowly being replaced by resolve, or maybe it was acceptance. I couldn't be sure. "I'm not following you. I come here every day to inspect the growing damage, and since I've been gone a few days, I came as soon as I made sure Ivy was okay."

Interesting when this island had nothing to do with his farm.

"There was a little boy here who told me King Zephyr did this because he was having a bad day. What did he mean by that?" I asked, even though I shouldn't care what the answer was.

Finn put his wings away and began walking. "Come with me."

I stayed unmoving. "Where are we going?"

"Do you always have to be so difficult?" he retorted.

I grinned. "I don't have to be, but it does come natural."

"Of course, it does." He quickened his pace, and I did the same while trying not to concern myself with why he was suddenly being nice to me. I'd already told myself no distractions. His change in demeanor shouldn't matter to me. To prove it to myself, I focused on our surroundings instead, trying to figure out where we were headed. Finn didn't seem the least bit worried about moving freely through the forest, and while I wasn't afraid, I wasn't stupid, either.

I had been exiled by the king, and I was on his land. If one of his guards came along and recognized me, things were going to escalate, and the plan I was beginning to get excited about would be ruined.

A few minutes later, there were still no signs of other fae, and we'd come to a ditch. Finn gestured toward it, but I wasn't sure what I was supposed to be seeing.

"Do you know what that once was?" he asked, and I shook my head. "It was a stream of water. One that was filled with freshwater instead of salty, courtesy of the king. It nourished the forest and provided water to the outlying homes, but when a family from this island dared to question King Zephyr after he killed their son, he cut the whole lot off. No one and nothing receives hydration out here unless they travel to the other islands to get it by the bucket."

"Why don't they leave? Seems stupid to stay where you're not wanted."

Finn ran a hand over his short hair, something I'd seen him do several times already and usually when I frustrated him. "You don't get it, and I'm not sure you ever will. Maybe this was a waste of time."

He turned to walk away, but I caught his arm. Power sparked along his skin at my touch, though I couldn't find the will to let go. All I'd been trying to do for the last day was fight whatever was building between us. With everything I'd been trying to sort out, I was tired of denying myself, even though I knew it was the wrong choice to make.

His silver eyes met mine, and he sighed. "You're only attracted to me because of what's running through my blood. Just ignore it."

"Maybe. Maybe not. I guess we'll never know.

Though, you can't deny you return the feelings. Our little tumble in the grass earlier proved that." I had no idea why I was reminding him of something I'd only done to throw him off. I didn't actually want him to *want* me, did I?

His hands gestured toward me, then he circled around so he was behind me. "I'm not blind, Lucinda. You're seductive, tantalizing, and my fingers itch to trace every inch of your skin." He paused, his breath hot on my neck, making me involuntarily lean into him.

"I wanted to rip that vampire apart when I saw his hands all over you the night I found you. A promise to my sister was the only thing that kept me from doing so." He backed away just when I thought we were moving beyond contempt.

He came back around to face me. "But none of that matters. Regardless of all the things that draw men to you—that made me want you no matter how badly I fought it—I see what lies beneath the surface. You are cruel, care nothing of the life around you, and think hurting other people is fun."

My eyes pinched together as an emotion I didn't ever experience tried filtering through, but I pushed it aside, knowing it was for the best. Finn showing up and declaring what I'd already known was not what I had planned.

You need to walk away. He will ruin you.

I knew the voice was right this time, but every time he was around, I learned something new. His comment about me only wanting him because of what was running through his blood made walking away even harder. The thought of showing Finn how hard that was for me was not acceptable, though. I had to do this my way before I lost myself.

Turning the tables on him and playing by my rules, I traced my fingers from his temple, through the light stubble along his jaw, and down his sculpted chest until I paused just above the top of his pants. "Listen, Finn. You need to quit thinking so much and just have some fun." The words were said more for me, but he'd never know that.

His hands circled around my waist and yanked me close enough that our noses were touching. "I don't do fun. I do serious, and there is nothing serious about you, Lucinda."

My fingers tapped his chest as I smirked up at him. "Oh, we'll see about that." Then, I backed a few feet away, needing space to breathe.

My thoughts were racing, and I knew if my plan was going to work, I needed Finn. I needed someone who was familiar to the lands and fit in to make the guards look one way while I was tearing down their king right under their noses. While I knew Finn was the worst choice for my wellbeing, I was also aware that he was the best choice given the situation.

I was going to have to let him in and accept the risk that there was something inside him that he was afraid of and could be screwing with me. Along with the risk that I could allow myself to care about more than just myself and Neva.

Keeping the elf safe was easy. She knew how to disappear into her pocket realms, but something told me Finn wouldn't do that, and if I let him in enough to help me, then there was no predicting what else might happen.

Was killing King Zephyr really worth allowing myself to care again?

As Finn patiently watched me, allowing me to filter through my thoughts, I knew I had my answer, but I would do my best to make sure I didn't change who I was. I couldn't let that happen, even if it made him hate me in the end.

"What are you going to do now?" Finn finally asked.

"I'm going to kill the king, but I need time. My plan won't be quick. It will be precise and done my way."

"Good. It gives me time to do what I need as well," he replied, much too happy with my answer.

"And what's that?" I asked.

His brow raised. "Do you actually care?"

"Not really. Just curious." I shrugged, already beginning to remind him who I really was.

He stepped even further away, then released his wings. "Well, for the sake of your *curiosity*, I'm going back to the house to get Neva. Then, we're headed to the castle."

Fury filled me within a moment. "Like hell you are. You're not taking her anywhere near that castle."

He grinned, and I didn't like it. I much preferred the tic in his jaw I usually caused. "Well, according to her, she finally got her sock."

I sneered. "That's not a real thing, you idiot. She's not my servant."

He leaned closer to me. "Exactly. Neva gets to do

whatever she wants, and since you left her, she wants to come with me to see where you're from. Oddly enough, she actually cares about you and still wants to help."

Emotions I wasn't used to slithered their way through me, and my chest tightened until I was gasping for air. I gripped the top of my corset, undoing buttons as I did. Breathing was getting harder by the second, and I bent over, trying to recover.

Sweat dripped off my forehead even though I was wracked with chills, and my body trembled like I was standing in the middle of the arctic instead of the perfect climate of Fae Islands. Dread coursed through me at the thought of King Zephyr getting anywhere near Neva. I couldn't control a single thought or action.

Finn's hand stroked my back as he spoke softly to me. "Just focus on breathing, Lucinda. One breath in, one out. Nothing else matters except those two things."

I listened to his words and did as he said, but it didn't work, and horror seized me all over again as my eyes darted around, paranoia taking over.

The king had found me, and he was slowly killing me, sucking every last drop of air from my lungs.

"Nobody is going to kill you. You're just having a panic attack, and you need to calm down before you pass out," Finn said, and I realized I must have said some of my thoughts out loud, but I didn't really care.

The tension in my chest refused to release its hold on me, but neither had Finn's touch. He continued to stroke my back, his fingers running from my hair line to my shoulder blades and tracing circles over where my wings extended from.

Every movement he made warmed my skin like never before, and heat pooled within me as I fought the doom and gloom with desire. Our unofficial partnership I decided on was about to take a turn I'd just sworn would not happen. I was losing control by the second and, for the first time since I was a child, my emotions took control of my actions.

My chest still ached, and that was something I'd have to deal with soon enough, but stopping the dread was my priority. Focusing on the desire between us, I stood up straight, my eyes finding his and seeing none of the contempt I was used to.

"All better?" he muttered, appraising me, but only making it as far as my chest where buttons still remained undone.

"Not even by a long shot." My hands grasped his shirt, and I jerked him toward me.

His eyes pinched together, but he didn't object, and his own hands tightened around my waist. I pushed my lips to his, not waiting more than a split second before my tongue was searching for his and my hands wrapped around his neck, avoiding the sharp points of his wings that were still extended.

My fingers traced over the hard edges as far as I could reach without breaking our kiss, and then moved inward over the leathery feel of his wings that I knew hardened just like my feathers did.

"This is wrong," he murmured against my lips.

"You've been living life all wrong if you think a woman pressed against you is anything but glorious," I replied and tilted my head back as his mouth moved down my jawline to my neck before finding what it was looking for in my chest.

Just when I finally felt like the heaviness in my chest was nearly gone, leaves crunched behind us. I peered between his wings to find Neva, Ivy, and a man I'd never seen before, all standing there with varying expressions. As much as I didn't want to stop what we were doing, I also didn't need Finn to go back to being perpetually pissed off at me.

I pushed back, letting my feet touch ground again. "We have visitors."

His body tensed as he pivoted on one foot, ready for a fight until he saw who was there. "What are all of you doing here?"

Ivy shrugged. "You're normally back by now. I thought you were in danger. Though, Neva was sure you'd just been preoccupied. I didn't believe her, and now I owe her five coins. Thanks for having no willpower, brother."

My eyes met Neva's, and I felt guilty that I'd left her, but she didn't seem upset with me. Instead, she seemed happier than I'd ever seen her.

CHAPTER 9

*B*efore I could focus too much on Neva's overly positive demeanor, I sensed someone watching us. The air was heavier, and based on the ominous feeling in my gut, I knew it wasn't the little boy I'd spoken with earlier.

My wings expanded and hardened as I took a step back from Finn and pushed out my magic. Teal swirls escaped my hands and blew through the trees, searching for whoever might be hiding away. I heard Finn hissing at the others to leave, but I didn't catch their replies.

The only thing that mattered was finding whoever lurked in the shadows before they got the chance to tell King Zephyr I was there. If I let the fae get away, I'd lose the advantage of surprise, and things would get much more complicated.

"Lucinda, what is it?" he asked, but I didn't answer as I focused on finding the direction of the intruder. For me, that was most important, but apparently, Finn didn't agree with my methods. "Damn it. This isn't just about you."

I ignored the pang in my chest as my feet moved of their own accord, further from those who could get hurt if the fae decided to attack. I was more than capable of taking care of this on my own, and that was the way I preferred it anyway.

Once I was further into the forest, my power latched on to the fae who was currently flying away from me, but he wouldn't be quick enough to get away. I pushed off into the air and stayed low, ignoring the shouts from Finn as I disappeared into the dying land.

Branches of the dead trees snapped off from the wind I was creating with my wings as I dashed in and out of the trees, but nothing fell fast enough to hit me. My wings extended and retracted in quick succession between obstacles. I was getting closer to the fae, but we were also nearing the edge of the forest.

If the fae made it beyond the tree line, I wasn't sure what we'd find, and it could mean trouble for me. I pushed another wave of power through my wings and finally had him in my sights. His wings were leather like Finn's, but tan in color. He wore the blue garb of a guard, and the memory of it gave me the last thrust of motivation I needed to catch up.

My arms wrapped around the fae, and we tumbled to the ground. His right wing made a cracking sound, telling me he wasn't experienced enough to have the reflexes entry guards should have. The king must have been getting desperate with his new hires.

The fae grunted beneath me. I threw a punch filled with magic, connecting with his jaw. "This is what happens when you put your nose where it doesn't belong."

"I didn't see anything. I don't even know who you are," he cried, but I didn't believe the pitiful quiver of his lower lip as I slammed another fist into his face, bruises forming before I even pulled away.

"Bullshit. Does King Zephyr know I'm here?" I hissed, trying to remain quiet since we were nearly at the edge of the forest.

He shook his head, but fury was consuming me, and I didn't trust him. The fae had to die. It was me or him, and he proved my point by bucking underneath me and nearly knocking me over. His left arm swung and missed my jaw by only a centimeter.

At least he wasn't pathetic enough to give up without a fight.

The fae tried to roll over on his right side, but his wing snapped again. "You probably shouldn't do that," I sneered and jabbed my elbow into his ribs, sending another shock of power through him at the same time.

He cried out and tried to hit me again, but I used my knee to pin down his arm. I wasn't in the mood to play with my catch.

My hands filled with dark magic and teal sparks flew from my palms as the center of them turned black. I brought my wings in, scraping the tips along his cheeks. "Your king is a selfish piece of shit, and you never should have taken his side," I sneered, lifting my hand to smash it into his chest.

"Lucinda, don't," Finn roared, and I glanced back at him. His silver eyes were all charcoal, and his wings were nearly black instead of the deep olive I was used to. "You don't have to kill him."

I shrugged, not understanding why he didn't see my side. "Yes, I do."

Turning back to the fae beneath me, he was sniveling like an idiot, and I didn't hesitate. My hand drove into his chest and I let my magic take over, sending it straight to his heart.

The fae's russet eyes widened as he choked, his mouth opening and closing, but no words came out, not even a final scream. I remained seated on top of him with my hand over his heart until I was satisfied that he wasn't going to get up again.

When I stood and turned around, Finn glowered at me. "You need to leave and never come back. There is something wrong with you, and we don't need your kind of help. We'll figure out another way."

He reached for Neva who was only a few paces behind him, but she shook her head. Finn nodded stiffly, then spread his wings and disappeared.

I glanced back down at the body and then at Neva. "What's his problem?"

Neva sighed and waved me over. "Come on, Lucy." She walked back toward the inner forest and I followed, seriously confused. My chest tightened again, but not as severe as before. When Finn had calmed me down, I thought we'd formed some sort of truce. Like maybe he was realizing I wasn't as bad as he perceived, but whatever had been there, even briefly, wasn't real if he could just walk away and not understand my intentions.

I caught up to her and asked again. "What is wrong with him?"

"I know it's hard for you to understand some emotions, but there's this thing called compassion. A lot of people have it, especially light fae. Finn didn't want you to kill that fae."

"But he was a guard. He would have gone back to the king and told him I was here. Then it would put Ivy at even more of a risk. Doesn't he understand I just did him a favor?"

Neva smiled softly, like she was speaking to a child. I tried not to be insulted but failed. "He would rather die himself than be the reason another innocent person is killed."

"That's the most absurd thing. Does he have no self-preservation?" There was something seriously wrong with these fae, and they were making my chest constrict with unknown emotions. If they weren't going to appreciate the fact that I just saved their asses, then they could piss off. I wasn't going to hang around so they could try and make me feel guilty for being the same person they sought out. Finn came to me for a reason, and he seemed to be forgetting that.

"Lucy, you were brought up by parents who did the king's bidding. They may not have worked directly for him, but they worshipped the ground he walked on. They cared for nothing but themselves and did whatever it took to increase their power and standing within the islands."

I snorted. "You talk like you know them. That's a pretty accurate description of my birth-givers. They were never parents to me."

"I don't need to know them. I only need to know you. I've listened to every word you've ever spoken. Little pieces of your life that you've mentioned. All of them I remember, and I put each fact together on my own to really understand who you are, even if you don't."

My eyes narrowed. This conversation was headed in the wrong direction. We were supposed to be plotting the king's death and celebrating the fact that there was one less guard for us to worry about, not trying to dissect the inner workings of my mind.

"Lucy, this is not your fault," she said, and I laughed hysterically.

"I know that. Why would you even say that? I've done nothing wrong. Killing that guard was the right thing to do."

She raised a brow and stopped walking. "Then why do you keep grabbing at your chest?"

I peered down and, sure enough, my fingers were rubbing my chest, just above my still-unbuttoned corset.

"You may not recognize it, but I do. A part of you, even if it's the smallest bit, is feeling guilty for killing that fae."

My head shook. That wasn't possible. Guilt was for

the weak, and I was anything but that. I was the perfect predator, and the choices I'd made kept me safe. How could that be so wrong?

Neva reached for me and took my hand. "Listen to me, Lucy." I hadn't missed all the times she'd called me Lucy, like she thought that would make her words get through to me easier. I wished I'd never asked her to, because it was actually working. "Whether you realize it or not, you've been searching for a reason to be different ever since you saved me in that alleyway."

My response was immediate and defensive. "No, that's just part of what I do. I punish those who prey on the weak, but what I'm best at is hunting down anyone for a price and I love it. Every part of it, but mostly when I get to watch them suffer."

"Yes, you do protect those who are too weak to do so themselves, but you don't normally take them into your home and give them a new life like you did with me. How about the last time you made someone truly suffer? Do you remember when that was?"

My fingers pressed to my temples. She was making me think too much, and my chest was getting tighter, so I focused on my breathing like Finn had told me to do until the pain eased. Once I was calm enough, I thought back and realized Dante the bloodsucker was the first one I'd attempted to toy with in more than a while, and I hadn't even really succeeded in that.

"What's your point, Neva? None of this changes who I am," I snapped.

She sighed. "I know you don't get it now, but I have

hope you will soon. My words won't change who you are, because you've already been changing on your own. You're just too afraid to admit it because it might make you vulnerable, and I accept that about you. It's why I've stuck around for so long."

"Bullshit. You had nowhere else to go," I replied, instantly feeling guilty for snapping at someone I considered a friend, but she was pushing me beyond my comfort level, and I didn't know how else to act.

"That's where you're wrong, Lucy. You might have saved me, but just because I was alone at the time, it doesn't mean I had no one in my life. I chose to stay with you, because *you* were alone, not the other way around."

I was done with talking, done with feeling, and, most importantly, done with people.

"I need to go. I've changed my mind and don't need to kill the king." Agony tore through me at the thought of leaving Neva in the forest by herself, making me hesitate before I left.

"Then go," Neva challenged.

"Do you want to come back to LA?" I asked, hoping she'd say yes.

She sighed again, something I'd caused her to do a lot as of late. "No. I'm going to go back to Finn and Ivy. They need help, and even if I'm not all powerful, I don't intend to let them fight either the poison or the king by themselves."

"You don't even know them."

"This is what makes the world go around. People helping people merely because it's the right thing to do.

It's what I've been trying to do for you, and I'll keep doing so, but right now, they need me more. I hope you'll stick around to see that as well."

She disappeared, leaving me alone, and for the first time since I was a child, I didn't like it one damn bit.

CHAPTER 10

This was bullshit. Complete and utter bullshit.

At some point after I'd chased after the guard, Ivy and the guy she was with had disappeared as well. So, I paced in the forest, moving away from the dead body I shouldn't care about. After seeing the upset from Finn and the disappointment from Neva, though, I didn't know how I felt.

I knew I wasn't okay. I had issues beyond comprehension, but for a while now, I'd believed as long as I didn't care about my problems or anyone else, then I could avoid the heavy stuff. Maybe I was wrong, or maybe I was just losing it.

Though, the stronger emotions were beginning to suffocate me. I kept trying to stuff it down, but they came back with a vengeance every time, partly in thanks to the people around me.

Just because I wasn't warm and fuzzy, didn't make me a bad person. I had good intentions. Well, most of the time.

Didn't that count for anything? Especially when their version of *good* seemed to be warped into some fairytale story that didn't actually exist.

The tortured look on Finn's face when I killed the guard made me want to prove him wrong. Sure, I knew I wasn't good, but what I'd done had been right. Good and right didn't always mean the same thing, and I was perfectly fine with merely being right.

They all expected me to leave.

Then, do it. You know it will be easier. You only need yourself to be happy. We can come back when you've forgotten about them. My inner voice said what I wanted to hear, but I knew it was wrong.

I had to stop King Zephyr. Even if it meant Ivy died in the process. Again, good versus right. Even Ivy had seemed to understand at least that.

Without overthinking my decision, I was determined this would be the final one, regardless of what happened next. I'd spent too much time over the last couple days being unsure about myself. It needed to end.

Instead of continuing to walk, I spread my wings and soared between the dying tree trunks until I saw water, then arced around and flew back onto North Island. I could have teleported myself back, but I spent this time with leisure, taking in the landscape.

On North Island, a creek wound between the farms and their crops were thriving, unlike the lands I'd just left behind on South Island. King Zephyr at least wasn't a complete idiot and knew he needed the fae on this island more than they needed him. He could afford to lose one food source, but not two.

The landscape varied from freshly turned ground to colorful crops and orchards. I found some more pomegranate trees and swooped down to snag another. They weren't common enough among the humans, and I was enjoying having them at my disposal.

My house growing up had one, and I remembered sitting underneath it with the animals and sharing the seeds. Well, until the falcon had come along. He'd poked holes in all of the fruit and tortured the animals until I'd decided enough was enough.

My birth-givers were just another example of people who didn't understand me. I didn't murder the stupid bird; I killed him in defense of the other animals and in preservation of my fruit tree. There was nothing wrong with that. If they'd only listened, they might have understood, too.

I hadn't seen them in over a decade, and I briefly wondered if I passed by them, if they'd even recognize me or I them. My face twisted. Gods, I hoped not.

When I arrived back at the Barlow farm, there wasn't anyone outside. I glided down to the dirt driveway and walked gingerly toward the house. Shouts could be heard, so I took my time and listened in.

"Even if we could convince her to come back, she's more likely to get you killed than save you," Finn grumbled.

"No, the king is going to get me killed. Whatever Lucinda does can only help. I'm pretty much dead already, so I'm prepared for the worst-case scenario. You need to go find her," Ivy responded.

"You're telling me you'd rather trust your life to someone who just killed a guard for no reason rather than your own brother?" His voice was even, but without needing to see his face, I could tell those words hurt him deeply to say.

Ivy sighed. "Listen, Finn. I love you and I appreciate you, but I am your older sister. Just because you're bigger than me doesn't mean you always know what is best. I know Lucinda is dangerous, but your judgement is clouded by the junk between your legs. I paid attention to her while she was here. The healer part of me tells me there is something good about her."

Oh, how I wished I could see the look on Finn's face right then. I imagined it changing from sun-kissed to red, then purple the moment Ivy said anything about him being attracted to me. Served the asshole right. He wasn't perfect and had no right to judge me for being different than him.

Feet shuffled and Neva spoke next. "Ivy is right. I've known Lucinda for two years now. Sure, she has her moments, but anything she does always comes from a good place. Maybe that doesn't sound like the Lucinda you heard about all those years ago, Finn, but I can assure you she's different now."

Ah, my little brownie elf. Always coming to my rescue.

If only she'd quit calling me out on my bullshit, I'd like her even more.

A thud sounded, and feet stomped on the old wood

floors. "Both of you are insane, but if this is what you want, Ivy, then I'll respect your wishes. Just remember when this all blows up in our faces, I tried to warn you."

Gods, he could be so thick-headed.

I slid around the corner, just in time to watch him storm out the door and fly off. I considered following him, but I was better off sticking with Ivy and Neva, given how erratic my emotions were.

My plans hadn't once stopped forming while I'd been uncertain about staying. I just needed to get Ivy and Neva on board before Finn returned.

TWO HOURS LATER, FINN STILL HADN'T COME BACK, AND I'd made no progress with Ivy and Neva. Ivy was all too excited that I'd returned and demanded we celebrate before we spoke about any plans. Except she didn't know how to handle her liquor and there would be no talk of killing the king until she was sober again.

"Have anutha," Ivy slurred, then hiccupped between giggles.

She thought with her vampire-like state she couldn't get drunk but was proved wrong after her third drink. I was on my fifth and only slightly buzzed while Neva was still sipping on her second glass.

I took the cup from Ivy as the fae wine sloshed over the edge. "Better me than you. I'm pretty sure you've had enough. Your boyfriend should be here to enjoy the perks." Drunk sex was the best kind.

Tears flooded her eyes as she sniffled. Oh Gods, no. I didn't do crying. When she'd told me about her boyfriend Maddox who hadn't been around much because he runs his own farm—he had been the guy with them earlier—she'd been practically glowing about him. So, I hadn't expected the mention of him to cause a breakdown.

"He wanna have my babies," she mumbled, and even though the words didn't quite go together, I knew what she was trying to say. "But I can't give 'em beebees." She hiccupped again, and Neva glared at me.

"This is your fault." She pointed.

I shook my head. "I didn't bring the wine out. Ivy did."

Ivy curled in a ball on the couch, murmuring incoherent words as I went to the kitchen to put the wine away. I wouldn't take care of a crying Ivy, but I'd at least make sure she didn't get any worse.

There was a window above the sink, and the moon was just rising in the sky. It was wintertime and even Fae Islands had shorter days like Earth.

As I observed the moon creeping higher into the sky, a flash of something caught my attention further into the orchard. My thoughts instantly began to turn. What if there had been two guards in the forest earlier and I'd missed one? Finn had me distracted, and I wasn't foolish enough to believe it wasn't possible for me to slip up, given everything I'd been going through.

Peeking into the living room, Neva was wiping bodily fluids from Ivy's chin, and I gagged silently before stepping away. I'd return before they even knew I was gone.

The back door opened without a sound and I stepped outside. The air was cool and crisp, and I took a deep inhale. Nothing triggered my senses except the scent of trees and fruit, but I headed where I'd seen the flash anyway.

It could have just been a glare from the moon through the glass, or it could have been the glint of silver from someone's blade. Either way, I needed to be certain. Not only for me, but for the people inside the house.

Ivy and Neva wouldn't be collateral damage to my past.

As I crept through the yard, I fleetingly wondered where Finn had run off to, along with Maddox. Ivy seemed head over heels with the fae, but it was interesting to me he hadn't been present more, considering I was around. He either had no idea who I was or didn't care much for the safety of his girlfriend.

Or, maybe he wasn't who Ivy and Finn thought he was. Everyone was suspicious to me, but there was also a possibility his farm really did take up most of his time and I was making a big deal out of nothing. I had at least tried to keep my thoughts away from believing he couldn't be trusted, but it didn't work very well.

A branch snapped up ahead, and I paused in the shadows of an outbuilding. I pushed my power out along the lush ground, hoping it would go unnoticed while doing what I needed it to do. Trundles of magic slithered from my fingertips, weaving between the blades of grass and around the trees.

Before they could get where I'd heard the sound, the repetitive thuds told me someone was running, and I wasn't about to let them get away. I cut off my magic and followed. I'd spent a lot of time in the home gym back at my apartment and running was as easy as breathing for me. So, with little effort, I caught up to the fae ahead just in time to watch his wings spread.

Oh, hell no, asshole.

I let my feathered beauties burst from my shoulders as I launched myself forward. He took flight, but so did I. This wouldn't be the first time I'd taken someone down in the air.

My wings were longer and stronger than his leather ones, so I gained on him easily. He was wearing all black, so I had no idea if he worked for the king or was just someone out lurking where they didn't belong. Either way, I was about to find out.

I lifted my palm and thrust magic into his back. His right wing buckled but recovered faster than I liked. Focusing back on getting closer, I increased my speed and decided this would need to be done hands-on.

He made the mistake of glancing back and slowed after seeing how close I was. My arms wrapped around his midsection as I brought my wings around his front and under his throat.

"Get us to the ground safely and I won't slice your head off," I demanded.

"Screw you," he spit right before a wave of electricity rolled through my body.

Son of a bitch. He had wanted me to catch him.

My hands released on instinct, and he shot higher into the sky. With sparks still rolling off my arms, I chased after him. Fury rose within me that I hadn't seen the move coming, and I was done playing games. This was why I liked to kill people who were up to no good. It required so much more effort to bring them in kicking and screaming.

Power built within me. I knew exactly what my next move would be, and the thought of the cries to come made me giddy.

When I was once again close, I didn't reach out. Instead, I sent a ball of magic into his back for a second time. This one wasn't meant to hurt, but to remove all sense of control over his own body. It brought me great joy to make grown men like him so weak and pathetic. I'd honed this particular skill for moments just like this.

He swiveled back to me as his wings slowed and arms fell limp at his sides. "What did you do?" he snarled, and I grinned.

"Oh, not much. Have a nice fall." I waved my fingers as his wings finally folded in and his dark eyes widened in fear of what was to come.

I might not ever know who he was or why he was spying on us, but at least he wouldn't be a problem anymore.

I flew down to make sure the job was done. I'd seen lesser men survive a drop like that, but not often.

When I got to the ground, the bastard was nowhere in sight. *Damn it.* Was he stronger than I'd given him credit for? There was no way. Not after the power I'd blasted him with.

I walked a few paces, trying to find where he landed, because it wasn't possible that his wings began working that soon after my paralyzing magic.

Except there was no dent in the ground, not even a disruption in the grass. There was literally nothing out of place.

"Are you looking for something?" Finn's voice sounded from behind me, and I swore to the Gods if he was holding on to that fae when I turned around, I would kill them both.

CHAPTER 11

Sure as shit, the fae I'd just hoped to kill was safely draped over Finn's arms like a baby. My lips lifted into a snarl. "What the hell do you think you're doing?"

He took a step back as I moved closer. "Keeping an innocent fae from dying."

This fae. I didn't know what to do with him. Too much of me still wanted him, especially as I watched the muscles beneath his black shirt strain with the weight of the fae. But other, likely smarter parts of me, were screaming he was bad news. He would never accept me for who I was. Or, who I thought I was.

"That fae was spying on us. You think I just randomly chase unknown supernaturals and kill them for the fun of it? I'm not a monster." Magic flickered from my fingers as my ire increased.

"You could have fooled me." He turned on a heel and headed back to the house, but I wasn't done with him.

I ran and didn't stop when we connected. I barreled into Finn and brought all three of us to the ground. The immobile fae landed underneath, and Finn rolled us off him.

"What are you doing?" he grumbled, blocking my punches.

"Kicking your ass for getting in my way." I feigned a left hook to his jaw and instead landed several punches to his ribs, each with added shock from my magic.

He groaned but didn't slow down. His legs wrapped around me, locking me against him, though my arms were still free.

I pulled up and dropped my elbow onto his throat while his hands were doing their best to restrain me without actually hitting me. This was why it didn't pay to be a nice person. His integrity was likely telling him it was wrong to hit a woman, but I wouldn't stop beating the shit out of him until I was good and ready, and he had every right to fight back. I'd have enjoyed it at this point in our non-relationship.

"You're being ridiculous, Lucinda."

My hands captured his and brought them above his head. "No, I'm not. I'm being cautious. It's kept me alive and at the top of my game for years now. Being as though I'm not the one with poison running through my veins, I'd say my method works better than yours."

He took advantage of my trapped legs and rolled us over again, and I couldn't stop the pleasure that filtered in when he took charge. Damn my stupid hormones.

"I'd rather die a thousand deaths than kill an innocent person."

He had my hands trapped, and I stopped fighting him. Unless I wanted to really hurt him with magic, I wouldn't win against his brute force.

His fingers loosened around my wrists. "Are you done now?"

"Not even close." I bucked my hips under Finn's, said a quick hello to the only part of him I liked, and then pushed him off me. Instead of continuing to attack him, I leapt for the unknown fae. Grabbing on to his collar, I jerked him up and pulled a small blade from the hidden pocket of my leather pants.

"Make one move and I'll cut his throat open," I said to Finn as he glowered at me.

"What are you doing?"

I traced the tip of the blade up the fae's cheek and enjoyed how his eyes darted between me and Finn, the only movement he was capable of until my magic wore off. "Well, like I said before, I'm not a monster and you probably did me a favor. Now that he's still alive, I can torture information from him. Like why he was here and who sent him."

The knife nicked the fae's ear, and blood dripped onto his shoulder, just missing my hand. I turned for the house and let the fae drag behind me, fully expecting Finn to follow.

A heavy sigh sounded from behind me, and Finn's footsteps finally began. "Not in the house, and I will be with you every time you want to speak with the fae. You're not to be alone with him. Not even for one second."

I tossed a glance back. "One of these days, I'm going

to…" I let the sentence trail off. Finn clearly wasn't ready for more. He might have thought so in the South Island forest, but I needed him to accept the darker parts of me before he got the fun bits. "Never mind. Just lead the way."

Finn strode ahead while I still dragged the fae behind me. His legs bounced on the ground as I took extra care to walk over every rock I saw. I followed Finn around the back side of the house and watched our surroundings as we moved. Where there was one cockroach, there were usually more.

But nothing stood out in the quiet of the night, and the moon was fully risen in the sky as we entered what appeared to be a small shed from the outside, but actually led to a set of stairs that took us underground.

Finn held the door open for me, and I raised a brow at him. "I didn't take you for the underground bunker type."

"Just because I'm not a murderer like you, doesn't mean I'm an idiot who thinks the world smells like roses."

I shrugged. I guessed that could be true. Instead of dragging the fae over the stairs, I tossed him down the steps. Finn hissed, but I grinned. "If he bleeds, it's not my fault. You should have carpeted the stairs."

He pushed past me, and I let him tend to the worthless spy while I took a peek around. The room was open, and I could see from one end to the next right where I stood. The walls were made from cinder with wood posts placed every ten-or-so feet for support to the ceiling. There was a couch with blankets on it and several chairs, one of which Finn had deposited the fae onto before moving to grab a rope.

"You like to tie people up, huh?" My brows waggled at him, but he ignored me, ruining my fun.

Gods, I was a glutton for punishment with this sexy fae. My mind wandered to the previous mention that the poison inside Finn was the only thing he thought attracted me to him. Given all that had happened, I was beginning to believe it might be true.

Over the course of the last few years, I'd refused to settle for less than I deserved. Not after how I'd been controlled by the king for so long. But now, I seemed to be throwing out my normal rules without a care. Finn didn't understand me, and he likely never would. Why was I still trying to get a rise out of him? It was just as much torture for me as it was for him.

I also needed to get back to my roots and remember all of the things that had kept me safe since I'd been on my own, torture being a key component. Oh, how much fun I'd had thinking of ways to torment the king without ever even touching him.

Finn grunted, pulling me from my thoughts, and I resumed taking in the bunker. Besides the couch and chairs, there was a small fridge and cabinet. I took the few steps across the concrete floor to open both only to find canned food and water. Why wasn't I surprised?

When Finn was done, I slid next to him, walking my fingers up his arm and giving his ear a slight tug. "Thanks for tying him up."

"I didn't do it for you, I did it for him." He met my heated gaze, the charcoal in his once again prominent. I licked my lips and enjoyed watching his eyes dart down to catch sight of my tongue before I patted him on the chest.

"You don't know him, right?" I asked Finn, realizing there was a good chance of that possibility.

Finn concentrated on our prisoner. "Never seen him before."

"Good. Now, it's my turn with him." I shoved Finn out of the way and placed my hand over the fae's chest, pulling my magic back out of him, so he could speak. "What's your name?" The fae sneered instead of answering. "How about I call you Dave? Dave sounds like a real douchey name I can deal with."

"You're both going to die." Dave spat the words in my face, and I turned my head toward Finn.

"Should I say 'I told you so' now or wait until he insults us some more?"

Finn stepped forward, nudged me out of the way, and grabbed the fae by his shirt. "What were you doing on my property?"

Dave merely smiled, refusing to answer. I latched my hand onto his leg and blasted him with something similar as to what he'd hit me with in the sky.

Finn released his grasp and cringed. Oops, I'd forgotten he was holding on to the intruder.

I didn't remove my hand until Dave cried out. "Answer Finn's question or there will be more of that and worse."

The fae growled at me, and I inhaled the scent of burnt skin before winking at him. "I bet that one's going to leave a mark."

"I won't let her hurt you if you answer the question," Finn said, and I snorted. Like he could really stop me.

Dave laughed as well. "She's right. You might as well kill me. I'll die before I betray my people like you have." The last bit was said with a scorned gaze toward Finn.

What had the sexy fae been up to that he wasn't telling me about?

"You don't know what you're talking about. I'd never betray our kind," Finn responded.

Dave leaned forward, straining against the ropes I assumed were magically bound. Finn couldn't be *that* naïve. "The proof is not only inside you, but right next to you. You brought her back and have doomed us all."

Dave's eyes closed, and he muttered under his breath as I sensed power building within him. I backed up and prepared for him to break free, excited to resume beating the shit out of someone. Finn didn't move, though. Poor fae still thought that good would always prevail. I hated to have to prove him wrong, but I would.

"What are you doing?" Finn demanded when Dave's body began trembling within the ropes. Sparks of magic popped from his skin, and blood dripped from his nose.

Well, this wasn't good.

"I'd back up if I were you, Finn," I called out, but he didn't listen.

I knew exactly what was happening, because I'd seen it once before. Dave had some big balls, I had to give him that. It took a lot of control to hold power in while it built until a point it literally burst from the body in an explosion. Considering this was about to get messy, and I had no desire to ruin my outfit, I moved back onto the stairs. Unfortunately, I only made it five steps before the fae exploded and bits of his body flew all around the room.

Finn was cussing like a sailor, and I just grinned as I glanced down. Blood spatter was on my boots, but thankfully they went up high enough that none of the filth landed on my clothes.

"I think now is the time. I told you so. Twice," I said, but Finn didn't reply as he charged toward the stairs, covered in blood and guts.

Well, there went my sex drive.

He was going to need at least three scalding showers before I would consider messing with him again.

I pressed myself against the wall as he passed by, completely ignoring me while mumbling to himself about psycho fae. I wondered if he was talking about Dave or me.

When I got back to the house, Finn was nowhere in sight and Ivy was passed out on the couch with Neva sitting at her feet.

"Finn just stormed through the house smelling like death. Do I even want to know what happened?" she asked.

I grinned. "A fae exploded on him. It was actually rather impressive."

Her face turned a little green. "That's horrid. How did that happen?" I told her the story, and her head shook. "We need to figure out what we're going to do. You can't just keep killing people. Sooner or later, the king is going to find out you're here."

My eyes met hers. "Oh, it's going to be sooner, and I already have a plan. Several of them, in fact."

"Care to tell me any details as to whatever it is you have already plotted?"

"In the morning. All you need to know for now is the king will suffer without me ever even touching him. Only when he's had his people turned against him and his sanity stripped away will he know who brought him to his knees."

CHAPTER 12

*A*fter Neva brought us temporary beds from her pocket realm, I'd slept like the dead for a few hours. A perk to being fae, we needed minimal sleep to be at our best. Well, unless that fae was Ivy and severely hungover.

"What the hell happened last night?" She groaned and held her head.

"You got drunk, unleashed a bunch of poison, almost got us all killed, gave us a strip show, then threw up everywhere. It was pretty epic." I smirked as she turned toward me, eyes wide.

"No, I didn't."

I shrugged. "Are you sure about that?"

Neva shoved my shoulder. "She's joking. Well, about most of it. You did throw up."

Ivy cringed as she stood, or attempted to, then hobbled back down the hallway.

I'd been awake since before sunrise, and Finn hadn't made an appearance. The mystery around him was taking up too many of my thoughts. The fact he appeared to want to hate me so much proved to be a challenge a part of me wasn't willing to walk away from.

The more I thought about him, the more I wanted that hate to turn into passion, nearly as much as I wanted to kill the king. Mostly, I was curious how much Finn was really holding back. But the risks involved if I couldn't keep emotions out of it were high. I still hadn't decided if the unknown rewards were worth the possible consequences.

"So, we didn't talk about the fae who showed up last night. The king must know you're here," Neva said.

"I doubt that, but he will soon enough." I paid close attention to my nails instead of Neva.

We'd slept in the living room, and Neva had already put our beds away. In their place was an additional chair I'd been wishing for since all of the other spots had been claimed around the room. I had no desire to stand every time we were here, and while the couch might have held one more person, it also appeared to be falling apart at the seams.

Ivy came back, appearing to have cleaned herself up, and sat in the rocking chair. "Is our furniture not good enough for you?"

"Nope," I deadpanned.

"Good to know." At least she didn't seem to get offended like her brother.

"Should we wait for Finn?" Neva asked.

Ivy squinted. "For what? What's happening?"

"Ms. Lucinda has a plan, and if we don't get it out of

her soon, then she'll put it into motion without us. I'd advise we get everything in the open right now."

Neva really enjoyed being right. Also, I didn't miss the fact she was back to calling me "Ms. Lucinda". Apparently, Lucy was only acceptable when I was being unreasonable and she was trying to soften me up.

"Well, then we don't wait. What happened to him last night anyway? I don't remember seeing him come back."

Neva chuckled and relayed the story. It was interesting hearing her version of it, much tamer than mine would have been.

"A fae was here? Trying to get you and my brother?" Ivy's face paled.

"It's not a big deal. We took care of it, but there will be more. This farm won't be a safe haven for much longer," I replied.

Her eyes closed, and her face turned beet red with sparks of magic flickering around her. I had no idea what was happening until Finn appeared right before her.

"What's wrong? Did someone hurt you?" he asked in a panic.

She punched him in the shoulder. "You need to quit being so damn nice and listen to Lucy. She is going to be the one to save us, and if your stubbornness gets in the way of that, I'll kick your ass myself. Do you understand?"

He backed up a few paces, his gaze moving between the two of us. "What the hell happened?"

"You tried to save a fae who didn't deserve saving." Ivy crossed her arms with a huff.

Finn rolled his eyes. "So, it's guilty until proven innocent now? You think the only way to win against the king is to stoop to his levels?"

She stuttered, but no words came out.

I stood and decided to pick up where she left off. "What she means is that you could have gotten us all killed last night by being too nice. Instead of refusing to believe that not everything is as you've always thought, maybe quit being an ass and open up to the idea not everything I am is evil."

Ivy held her fist up. "That's right."

I connected mine with hers before smiling sweetly at Finn and sitting back down.

The twinge in his cheek just above his jaw was back in full force as he sat next to Neva. "How do you do this?"

Neva wrapped an ebony curl around her finger. "Ms. Lucinda is right. While I don't always agree with her methods, she is your best chance at making it out of this mess alive. All of you."

Finn tossed his head back. "I'm surrounded by too many women. Where's Maddox? He'll see my side."

Ivy snorted. "If he knows what's good for him, he'll agree with me."

Yep, I definitely liked the sister. At least for the day.

The door opened and Maddox entered as if he'd been summoned like Finn. "Of course, I'll always agree with you my love." Maddox went to her and kissed her cheek before kneeling beside the chair. "What did I miss?"

She squeezed his shoulder. "Try to catch up and I'll explain the rest later. I want to know what Lucy has planned."

Maddox nodded, his hazel eyes taking me in as he pushed his shoulder-length brunet hair behind his ear. There was a slight bend to his nose, and I wondered what else he did besides tend to his farm.

Meanwhile, Finn grumbled some more, but I ignored him and stayed standing. Nobody ever got anything done by sitting on their ass.

"Before we get into my plans, I need you to tell me more about this poison or sickness you've taken on," I said to Ivy.

She brushed back blonde hair that was similar to her brother's but where his was dark, hers was strawberry. "Well, when the king came to me, his skin was ashen, and he'd aged several decades. To be honest, I didn't even recognize him at first. His guards practically carried him in, and that should have been my first sign to refuse."

"He would have killed you on the spot for treason if you had, so you probably made the right choice. For as long as he lives, you get to live. If you hadn't come to me, that could have been decades more. What's wrong with that?" I asked, because who didn't want to be forever young without having to be weak to blood like the vamps?

"Considering I was engaged and wanted to have a

family, everything is wrong with *that*," she replied gruffly.

Maddox held her hand. "You're still engaged. I'm not going anywhere."

She huffed. "That's a conversation for later."

I must have made a face at their affection, because Ivy scowled at me for the first time.

"Easy, sis. Lucinda here doesn't know what love is, so you'll have to excuse her ignorance on things that are important to most people," Finn said, calming her down, and I winked at him.

"But I know what desire is." I might have made the joke, but I didn't miss the way my chest ached at his words. He was right, and I hated it.

His hands curled around his knees, and I turned back to Ivy. "So, you're going to risk dying early so you can live? I don't understand why you don't just do whatever you want now."

"Because what I want is a life with Maddox and the babies I've dreamt of, but I won't be with him and break his heart by not being able to give him everything he deserves."

Oh, kill me now. We'd entered territory I had no wish to be in.

"Back to the king. What did he tell you?" I asked before my lack of empathy upset her again.

Ivy wiped a stray tear from her cheek. "He said he'd been struck with some sort of flu, and his weakened immune system couldn't fight it, but he was certain a young, powerful healer like myself could do the job. Later, I'd found out he was working his way through a list of known healers and had already killed more than a dozen before he arrived on our doorstep."

None of that surprised me in the least.

"As I took the sickness from him, I realized too late that it wasn't natural." Ivy's hand covered her heart. "There is a darkness that lives within my heart now. I don't know where it's from or what it could do, but I've lived with it for nearly two years and I'm done."

I moved closer, lifting my hand. "Do you mind?"

She shrugged. "Have at it. I doubt anything you do can make it worse."

I grinned. Oh, how naïve she was. Things could always be worse.

My palm pressed against her chest, and she moved her hand away. As soon as my fingers touched her skin, I was instantly drawn to the power within her. There was a heaviness about the darkness within her that I didn't recognize, but I wanted it for myself, regardless. There was no way this could be poison. No, it was more than that and I wanted to know what.

I closed my eyes, and my hand burned against Ivy's skin as she flinched beneath me, but I ignored her discomfort. She was wrong. The magic within wasn't contained in her heart. It flowed through her blood and to every point in her body.

"Lucinda, I think that's enough," Neva said from somewhere behind me.

"Just another minute."

A strong hand tugged on my free arm. "Neva's right. Let Ivy go."

"I said I'm not done yet," I snarled, and Ivy squealed beneath me.

Within a second, my hold on her was broken, and I went flying across the room until my head connected with the wall. I didn't have to see myself to know that my eyes were glowing teal and my wings were spread. "You shouldn't have done that."

Finn stood in front of Ivy. "You don't scare me." Magic built in his palms, and I welcomed the attack. After touching the power inside Ivy, my adrenaline was on fire. I needed a release.

Kill her and take the power. You'll feel even better, the sinister voice inside me cooed, sounding more comforting than ever before. As I considered the option, I knew it was the wrong one, but that didn't stop me from wanting to listen.

Maddox moved in front of Ivy, and Neva stepped between me and Finn. "Enough. You two need to get it together before you get us all killed. Ms. Lucinda, that poison is meant to lure dark fae. If you absorb too much of it, you will die."

I tilted my head toward her. "How do you know?" From what I had just experienced, the consequence should be the exact opposite.

"I'm neither light nor dark. I'm merely a brownie elf who was born to serve, but it doesn't mean I know nothing about magic. When I met Finn, something within him repelled me. I thought it reminded me of you because it is dark, but that's not it at all."

Finn moved closer to her. "What is it then?"

"You have trace amounts of the poison within you,

and it's not enough to kill you or another supernatural. But it is enough to harm someone. Whatever you did to yourself to be able to syphon some of that dark magic may never go away." Neva's eyes softened, then she moved her attention to Ivy who was muttering incoherently and had tears trailing down her face.

Neva wiped them away. "This is not your fault."

"Yes, it is. I should have just let them kill me, and then the king would be dead, and everyone would be better off."

"That's the second biggest lie you've ever said," Maddox grumbled, and Ivy's sobs got louder. So much for thinking she was full of snark. That side of her I could tolerate, but this hungover emotional part of Ivy was too much. An unease settled within me at the sight of her tears, and I didn't know what to do with it.

Maddox glowered at me, then picked Ivy up before carrying her out of the room. An awkward silence settled over the remaining three of us, and I retracted my wings before deciding to take a seat. I held my palm out and channeled my energy, looking for anything to tell me more about what I'd just felt, but there was nothing out of place.

No marks, no extra magic, no nothing.

Well, except for the fact the darkness within me was fighting harder to come out. Whatever poisonous magic was in Ivy, it was strong enough to awaken mine like nothing before it.

As soon as I'd touched her, the power inside her clung to me and drew me in. I licked my lips as the thought of that much energy fueled the darkness inside me. My thoughts were at war with one another and, for once, I wasn't certain which was right.

After that experience, I understood how vampires felt when they needed blood and probably how King Zephyr had become subject to the poison.

Knowing him, he would have thought it was power to be controlled—just like I'd allowed myself to believe, or maybe even still believed. He would have been greedy, taking all that he could as quickly as possible. I was on the same path until Finn had ripped me away.

Whoever created the magic knew him well. If only they had been successful, then the poison would have done its job and I wouldn't be in this mess.

Their failure didn't matter, though. I would finish what they started, and King Easton Zephyr would no longer rule Fae Islands.

By the time I was through torturing him, he'd be going straight to hell.

CHAPTER 13

Finn and Neva were in the midst of a completely different conversation once Ivy had been carried away by Maddox. I'd missed most of it while I'd been busy with my internal thoughts that were easier for me to process than their emotions. Now it was time to reveal my plans.

"There is a spot by the for—" Finn was saying, but I cut him off.

"We're going to begin terrorizing the king tomorrow. This will be a three-step plan, each piece more important than the last. The two of you will have to remember there's a difference between right and good if you're going to be part of this, because it's either my way or you're on your own."

Finn's chest rumbled. "I was talking."

"And?"

He shook his head. "You're impossible. What are these steps you've managed to come up with all on your own?"

Well, at least he wasn't stupid enough to argue with me.

"The first is we need to get the people still loyal to him to begin questioning his ability to keep them safe and fed. There's about to be a shortage of fresh water and food."

"Won't that harm the innocent?" Neva asked.

I shrugged. "Some will get sick, but nobody should die. At least, I don't think."

She sighed heavily but didn't say anything else.

"And after that?" Finn asked.

I sat back down in my new chair and kicked my feet up over the side. "Then, there will be a mental attack. I'm going to use a spell I acquired back in LA to make the king so paranoid that his closest guards even begin to doubt his soundness. Especially when one-by-one they begin to disappear."

Finn scoffed. "And you think you can pull all of this off on your own?"

"Well, that's a stupid question." I turned toward Neva. "While I dumb things down for pretty boy, will you go to your little pocket realm and find my weapons, along with my trunk of spells?"

She nodded. "Of course, Ms. Lucinda."

Finn sneered as soon as she disappeared. "You're ridiculous making her do things for you like that."

I sat up straighter. "Did you ever take a moment to consider that maybe I gave her a purpose? Do you know anything about Brownie Elves? She was born to assist, and when I found her, I saved her life. She owes me nothing for doing so, but she stays because she enjoys it. Maybe stop being a dick about it and get over the fact I'm not as horrid as you thought. It's clear as day that you hate to think you might have been wrong about me."

A look of surprise passed over his face, but it was gone just as quick as it came. "Whatever."

"I really don't understand you. If I didn't know any better from our previous, more friendly interactions, I'd maybe wonder if you were anti-cooch and pro-boner. Maybe you're both? No judgement here, but it definitely changes things if we're playing for the same team."

He choked on air, his face turning several shades of red. Yeah, I'd been hanging around the humans for much too long and their odd names for body parts were quite entertaining.

"What the hell did you just say?" he wheezed.

I waved my hand in the air. "You know you've been resistant toward me. Maybe it's because I'm not packing the right kind of—"

He held his hand up. "Enough. I'm very much into women. I just prefer them to care more about others than you do. I thought I could ignore that detail at one point, but watching you mercilessly kill the fae in the forest showed me that likely wasn't something I could ever be okay with."

I merely stared at him, unsure of how to respond. He'd just confirmed what Neva had tried to say and what I'd been thinking about already, but for some reason, that didn't make me feel any better.

"What's step three?" he asked, giving me the distraction that I needed.

"Step three is the attack. After parts one and two, the king should be left weak in the mind and without an army. Or at least, not one the size he has now. Killing him won't be easy. He's been spelled to live forever, and while I won't necessarily wait for Ivy to be free of the poison she took on, it would be helpful in finding a way through the enchantments he was gifted at coronation."

Along with being spelled to never lie to his people, any ruling leader was enchanted with long life and resistance to most things that could kill the rest of us fae. Whoever had nearly ended him before was smart, and I was surprised they hadn't tried again.

"It's a good plan."

It was my turn to choke. "Excuse me? Did you just actually agree with me?"

"I'm sure we won't agree on how you execute each of those steps, but the general idea of them is doable. It creates the least number of casualties."

I snorted. "It will also drive the king to insanity. It will break him mentally. Who cares about anything else?"

"I do," he snapped.

I turned in the chair and put my feet on the ground, leveling my gaze on him. "Just remember, at some point, it's going to come down to making a choice that will either save your sister or get someone else killed. When that happens, I bet my right versus good will make a hell of a lot more sense, and I'll be happy to tell you 'I told you so' once again."

He stood from the couch. "I need to go clean the bunker."

I blew him a kiss. "Try not to get blood on your clothes again."

He ignored me and slammed the door on his way out. Hopefully, some time with minced fae body parts would make him realize I wasn't as bad as he was making me out to be.

Or maybe you're worse, my inner darkness reminded me.

Maybe I was.

SOMETIME LATER, I WAS DRESSED FOR THE DAY IN A COLOR I hadn't worn since I was last on Fae Islands: navy blue. The king thought his people should all wear similar colors to show unity, but I had always thought it was more about seeing just how far he could control everyone.

From what I remembered, only those on West Island, or visiting fae, wore the bland color. So, if I wanted to blend in, then that was what I needed to do as well. I wasn't ready for King Zephyr to know I'd arrived. He needed to suffer beyond comprehension before that happened.

Neva arrived with two trunks. "This should be most of it. I can go back for more if you're looking for something more particular."

"I'm not sure what I'd do without you," I said honestly.

She grinned. "You'd make a mess of things and have to kill a lot more people."

She wasn't wrong. It had been my life before stumbling upon her.

"Where is Mr. Finn?" she asked, glancing around the living room.

Neither him, Ivy, nor Maddox had returned, but I didn't mind. Some time apart for all of us was probably a good idea.

"Last I heard, he was cleaning up fae guts from his bunker," I replied.

She shook her head and sighed.

"What?" I asked, knowing I shouldn't.

"Nothing." She bent toward one of the trunks, but I walked to her and kicked it away.

"You're not a slave, Neva. Say your piece."

She nodded curtly and met my gaze for a moment before stepping back and taking a seat on the couch. I did the same, but across the room in my comfy chair.

"So, what has you disappointed in me this hour?" I inquired.

"I'm assuming you'd like me to be frank?" I nodded and she continued, "Well, it's not disappointment. It's frustration."

I chuckled. "How do I frustrate you, little elf?"

"Over the last couple of weeks, even before Finn arrived, you've been changing. You're not happy, and when you find something that could change that, I can see how much you want it, but instead of taking the chance, you attempt to destroy it. Even the little things like the flower stand you nearly destroyed after a happy couple stood beside you gushing about their engagement. That sort of reaction isn't normal."

I wanted to laugh and snarl at the same time. She had no idea what she was talking about.

"It's very normal for me. I'm a dark fae. The warm and fuzzies won't ever be something that makes me happy. Destroying, taking justice no matter the cost, and having no remorse for my actions is who I had to be to survive my life under the king's roof. While he doesn't control me any longer, I can't change who I am because of my time spent there, and neither can you."

She smiled softly. "I know I can't, and I didn't stay with you so I could. I stayed with you, because I can see the war you fight within yourself and I want to be there when the winner is chosen. Because if I'm right, no matter how bad it gets before it's over, the hell you'll go through will be worth it."

I laughed again, more like cackled. "Oh, Neva. How I wish I could live in your fantasy land. Regardless of why you made your choice, I will admit, I'm glad you stayed."

She didn't smile or laugh with me. She didn't even shake her head like normal. The elf merely stared at me in disappointment.

"What?" I bit out when she didn't look away.

"Maybe I'm wrong, but I really hope I'm not."

Her words lit a fire within me, and my ire rose. I stood and stalked toward her while magic spilled from my pores, and my wings extended as the hold on my control diminished.

"I'm done, Neva. I've been nice because I care about

you, but if you try to guilt me into being something I'm not, you won't like who I become."

By that time, I was in her face, but she didn't even flinch. Instead, she lifted her eyes, challenging me. "I'm not sure you would, either."

Before I said something that I couldn't take back, I turned on my heel, pulled my wings closer, and stormed out the door. My anger was at an all-time high, but I ignored who it was really directed at. If I dug too hard into the emotions I didn't really understand, then I would be forced to face the things I'd put off for so long.

Neva had a way of trying to make me see things in a different light, but now was not the time. I couldn't afford to break down my very core of who I'd been for years right when I was supposed to rely on myself to kill the king.

Even if I wanted to change, even if I thought it wasn't the worst idea to explore whatever had been going on inside me lately, I couldn't do that and complete the task before me.

Once outside, I threw my hands in the air and let the rumble in my chest build into a snarl before considering a long healthy scream. I paced the yard, then made my way toward the orchards. I needed to be alone and clear my head.

I'd agreed to help, and I was a fae of my word. Out of all the bad I'd done in my life, I'd never once backed out of a commitment, but damn if I didn't want to right then.

Fly away and don't turn back. It's not too late. We will regroup and come back to finish without distraction.

Gods, I wanted to murder that voice. It had always been lingering, but it had gotten more demanding lately. Nothing like having an inner voice that drove me batshit crazy.

My wings were still out and twitched with the need to soar in the sky, but I knew that if I did that, I'd end up listening to that voice. I'd never come back.

I had enough demons on these islands to smother; I didn't need to create more by giving up when things got complicated.

That was all this was, a complicated situation I just needed to simplify. No more friends. No more playing nice. No more pushing that sexy fae to his breaking point. I'd come here for a job, and that was what I needed to focus on. Nothing more, nothing less.

Just as I'd begun to calm down, leaves crunched from behind me. I shot a stream of magic out of my hand as I turned around, uncaring who might be in my path. If they were stupid enough to approach without making themselves known, they deserved to be zapped.

My teal magic arced around Finn as my eyes took him in. His shirt was off, and he had blood smeared above his arched brow. His eyes glowed around the edges, and I lost myself in the depth of charcoal for a moment until he stalked toward me, his intent becoming clear.

"What are you doing, Finn?" I asked.

He grunted and mumbled, but I didn't understand a

word. With every step, the gap between us closed. After my revelation just literal seconds before, I knew I should back away. Finn wasn't angry with me. He had a hunger in his eyes I'd certainly seen before, though never like this with him. This wasn't how it was supposed to go. I was going to leave the sexy fae alone. I was going to do my job and get the hell away from these people who made me feel.

Then, Finn's strong hands wrapped around my upper arms, and he tugged me against him. "I'm done letting you have the upper hand."

CHAPTER 14

While I'd been aware Finn was sexy as hell, I hadn't known how deliciously sinful he could be until he took real control. His fingers grasped my jaw, his palm pressing just above my neck, and his eyes turned black a split second before his lips captured mine.

Without waiting for permission, his tongue demanded entry, and I eagerly reciprocated while his other hand tangled in my iridescent hair, angling my head to deepen the kiss. Though there were small parts of me that screamed to pull away, I wasn't missing this.

My wings relaxed, and I pressed closer, enjoying the heat our combined bodies created and the feel of his slicked skin under my palms as I explored him with abandon. My right hand moved around to grab his ass while the other held on to his shoulder. My back ended up pressed against a fruit tree as Finn took what he wanted from me.

Once he was done exploring the depths of my

mouth, his lips replaced his fingers as he ventured across my jaw. Light stubble along his face scratched against mine while his hand stayed around my neck, keeping me in place with just enough pressure that I didn't feel threatened, only aroused.

As he continued his journey, Finn's teeth nipped at my shoulders, causing bumps to rise along my exposed skin. Then, he gazed hungrily back up at me. His eyes were still black, and I realized that wasn't a good thing. Not even for someone like me.

That knowledge was like a bucket of ice water being thrown on us, and my senses returned to normal. Whatever darkness was inside him had taken over and, while I preferred this side of Finn, it couldn't be controlled from the outside.

I raised my hand to smack reality back into him, but he'd seen the move coming and caught my wrist. "I don't think so, Lucy. Aren't you having fun?"

"That I am, but you're done." If I couldn't hit him, I'd zap him. With my right hand still on his ass, I sent a stream of power right through his jeans, scorching him until he backed away.

"What the hell, Lucinda?" he roared, then glared at me with the silver back in his eyes where it belonged.

"I was just thinking the same thing. Care to tell me what happened just now?"

He glanced around, and then down at himself. He was shirtless and rocking an impressive hard-on. "What did you do to me?" he snarled.

I waggled my finger at him. "I was out here minding my own business when you came to me. You either let the dark magic in you take over, or your beaver-basher has more control over you than your brain does."

His head tilted up toward the sky, and he closed his eyes while pacing several feet. "What happened?"

"Like I said, I was out here minding my own business. You found me, then kissed me like your life depended on it, and I zapped you once I realized you weren't fully in control. But let's be honest, even if you weren't fully aware, you've obviously been wanting to do so." My eyes darted toward his junk, and he adjusted himself so the hard-on wasn't *as* noticeable.

"How did you know I wasn't in control?" he asked.

"Your eyes. They were black instead of charcoal like they normally are when you're all riled up, but they're not anymore. More silver than anything. You're going to have to keep your shit together, or you're going to get someone killed. Or possibly laid, but that's not actually a bad thing."

Okay, I was lying to him and myself. The latter was a bad thing. It made things complicated, and I needed to focus on the task of killing King Zephyr and nothing else.

Not even lickable fae.

Damn, he really needed to put a shirt on.

"Listen, Lucy. We can't do this. It's not a good idea."

He'd used my preferred name, and he wasn't speaking down to me. It was a rare instance, but I had to agree with him.

"You're right."

His eyes widened. "Seriously?"

"Don't be so shocked. Like I've said several times,

I'm not a monster. I know how to be reasonable, and before you accosted me, I'd already decided the same thing. Though, unlike you, when a sexy fae wants to show me a good time, I don't usually say no."

He sighed, my comment clearly reminding him just who I was. "I'm going to go get cleaned up."

As he retreated, I watched the muscles of his back, finding myself glancing lower and enjoying the view of his ass cheek where I'd burned through his pants with my magic. "You might want to throw those pants away, too, unless you enjoy a little breeze."

He stopped, shifted ever so subtly, then his shoulders curved in defeat before he began walking as fast as he could go without running. I chuckled at his response and straightened my own clothes. Since everyone else was busy, maybe it was time for me to act.

If I was going to follow through on my word, it was time to put my plans into motion. The first step required stealth, meaning I didn't need Finn or anyone else joining me. It was nearing lunch time, and I needed to hurry if I wanted the effects of step one to happen before dinner.

A piece of my hair whipped across my face, reminding me that I wasn't exactly one to blend in to a crowd with my unique hair color. Unfortunately for me, I wasn't born with the ability to change my physical features. I could draw out inner beauty like I did with Neva and magic clothes, but transforming body parts was beyond my capabilities.

I was going to need help.

As I headed back to the house, I saw Ivy and Maddox heading in. I wasn't in the mood to deal with their lovefest, so I held back, thinking about the items Neva brought back and if there was anything in there that would help me.

Another few minutes passed, and I still had no ideas on how I was going to walk through West Island without being recognized. Then, Maddox exited the house and spotted me. I'd hoped since he didn't really know me, he'd just keep walking, but no such luck.

"Can you really save her?" he asked gruffly.

"No, but if any of you realized there is another whole world just beyond this realm, you'd know it is filled with supernaturals who probably can. Like I told Ivy and Finn, spells aren't my thing, but I can, and will, kill the king."

He stared me down. "Even if it kills Ivy?"

"Haven't you heard? I'm an uncaring monster," I said sarcastically, even though part of me wanted it to be true. Caring left room for vulnerabilities that could hurt me. "Whatever consequences come from the king's death don't matter to me. Ivy apparently doesn't care either. I was asked to kill the king, and that's what I'll do." And that was the truth I needed to keep at the forefront of my mind as I moved forward.

"Speaking of," I continued. "I need to do something, but I don't want anyone to recognize me. You don't happen to know a fae trustworthy and capable of giving me a bit of a make-under?"

Maddox frowned. "Make-under?"

I moved my hand down my body. "Obviously I

don't need a make-*over*. I need to be bland and blend in. This face isn't forgettable." I'd learned that several times over since I'd hit maturity eight years ago. Sometimes it was a good thing, and others, not so much.

He nodded. "I see. Well, you're in luck. I can actually help with that. I'm not the best at it, but my mother was, and I inherited the trait from her."

No, he didn't have… Oh, he really did. My surprise was clear. He seemed so similar to Finn that I'd expected leather wings to sprout, but that was not at all what I caught sight of.

An interesting mix of blue and green gossamer wings spread from his back, and he held his hand up, fingers wiggling as magic arced around them. "Want me to give it a try?"

I nodded, taking in the thin wings that looked weak, but I knew were nothing of the sort.

As he inched closer, his hand still swirling with magic, he paused. "You swear to kill the king, no matter the consequence, if I help you?"

I eyed him. There was something about the fae I wasn't liking. He said nothing of his betrothed. His only concern was for the king's death. That was more than interesting to me. For now, I'd let it slide, but there would be no trusting Maddox beyond the use of his abilities. Even that was risky, but I didn't really have a choice at that moment.

"Of course. I'm a fae of my word," I replied easily. That was one thing I could never doubt.

He closed the gap between us and placed his palm

over my forehead. My eyes shut as soothing magic overtook me, and I wanted nothing more in that ten seconds than to take a nap under the sun.

When Maddox pulled away, he grinned. "That should do the trick."

I didn't have a mirror, but I pulled my hair forward. It was the same length, but more of a mousey brown color with no shine. My hands felt my face, yet nothing about it felt different. "What did you do?"

"It's not a physical change, Lucinda. It's a glamor. You're still you. The eyes are just tricked into seeing something that's not really there. Go find a mirror if you don't believe me."

I didn't have time to do that. If I went back into the house, the others would ask too many questions. I just needed to trust he wasn't screwing me over.

"And you won't tell them I'm leaving?" I asked.

"So long as they don't ask me directly. I won't lie to Ivy and Finn. They're my family."

Interesting. That was the first thing he'd said that really made me believe he cared for them.

"Fair enough. I'll be back in a couple of hours. How long should this last?" I really didn't want to be standing in the center of the market and have it fade away.

"It will last as long as nobody else injures you with magic, and you can make it go away any time you'd like by placing your palm where mine was and zapping yourself. Or, I can do it for you when you're back. Whichever you'd prefer." He shrugged as if he didn't care, but I could see the smirk hiding. He'd enjoy that a little too much.

"I think I can manage."

He nodded, and I moved away, not giving him my back until there was at least ten feet between us. Then, I spread my wings and flew. I glanced back to find Maddox already gone. I couldn't decide if I was more hopeful that he would turn out to be a sneaky bastard I got to kill or if I would be wrong so I could keep using his skill set.

That was a problem for the future. For now, I needed complete focus on the present. I hadn't been to the castle and marketplace in over three years. Things could have changed, and I needed to blend in. So, there was no room for error in the moves I made.

If I was successful, then I would be out of there within an hour, but I wasn't naïve enough to believe I'd have no issues.

As my wings flapped faster and harder than they had in a long time, I couldn't stop the smile that graced my face as I pictured my victory over the man who once tried to break me.

CHAPTER 15

When I arrived at West Island, I'd thought there would be some sort of fear or dread taking over, but instead, there was only glee. The darkness inside me—that had been seemingly out of control as of late—was even at ease as we flew closer and landed on the ground. Though, I wasn't sure that was a good thing.

The king's island was mostly tropical. No crops were grown here, and it reminded me more of a resort than a land for the people. The castle was opal and obnoxious. Though, even with the bright exterior color, there was an ominous feeling about the structure with its dark roof, turrets, spires, and many windows that only allowed for seeing out, not in.

I could only make out the tops of the turrets as I walked through white sands, then onto grass as I pulled my wings in. I needed to leave those hidden at all costs. Other feather-winged fae like me didn't live by the king's laws, only the few that the reigning supernatural council enforced. There were no second chances with them, and I was glad I'd never been on their radar before.

The other fae with wings like mine were more nomadic than anything. While I had a strong dislike for most people, I still preferred to be among other magical beings, living life freely.

As soon as I was within the confines of the small tree forest around the island, I checked my pockets. I had a dagger for discreetness if needed. I had two vials from the trunk with a spell that would make a fae sick. Lastly, I made sure my blue attire was in place.

My pants were loose to hide the items I carried, and the top was tight to show off my curves. Fae weren't prudes, so it would have called attention if I tried to blend in "too" much.

Once I was sure there was nothing left to chance, I exited the tree line and headed for the main gate.

West Island wasn't open to all like the other land masses. The guards monitored every fae in and out of the marketplace. Lucky for me, I had a few other identities that would pass their questioning, but each of them could only be used once and needed the glamor Maddox had provided.

The brick wall curved around, and a guard spotted me. I kept my head up, acting as if I belonged there. He stepped out from his post, no weapon in hand, but his metal-grey leather wings were on full display.

"What brings you to the castle today, miss?" he asked politely, but I could see the suspicion in his russet eyes.

Using my best British accent, I replied, "I'm visiting from England. I try to come here once every few years and visit the markets, but I will admit, it's been a while. I see things have changed some since I was last here. Do I need to request a visit and come back?"

Pretending to be okay with not being invited in would hopefully ease any distrust. It wasn't uncommon for some fae to live outside of the realm.

"What is your name?" he asked, pulling out a small device.

"Maribel Justad. I was born from parents that lived on East Island, but they had a falling out with my uncle before I was born, and I've never lived here."

When the guard searched for Justad, he would find three fae with that last name. All three dead. All three by my hand.

"Where are your parents now?" he asked while keeping one eye on me and the other on the screen.

I grabbed at my chest, sighing. "They were attacked after my uncle requested their presence several years back. It's why I haven't been back in so long. This place is painful for me."

He nodded, and I knew he was confirming every detail on that screen. The king was a psychopath, through and through. He had information on every fae who'd ever lived on these lands.

"Well, it doesn't appear your parents ever registered you. I'll just need to get your information and you can enter." He held up the device and took a picture of me. Too bad for them, I'd never look like this again.

He asked evasive questions about my medical and

family history, all of which I made up answers to, and then had me sign my name. "Next time you come back, this won't be an issue. Thank you for not being difficult. Your kind don't usually care for the questions."

Ah, my kind. Dark fae. Not even the glamor could hide who I really was.

Instead of replying, I merely smiled and walked past him. Another guard pressed a button and the titanium gate unlocked. Pushing through, I didn't hesitate and enjoyed the sound of the locks reengaging.

My first stop would be the well. That was the main water source for all of the people who lived within the walls of West Island. I had two vials of the same spell; one of them would be used on the well, while the other would be snuck into the food at the individual stands in the market.

There was a line at the well, and I stole a bucket on my way. Fae chatted idly around me, none seeming to be hating their life, and I wondered if Finn had been lying when he mentioned the loyalty on West Island being weak.

But as I glanced around, I slowed my gaze, really focusing, and found the changes. More guards roamed the streets. Fae smiled, but when I looked closer, I could see the strain in their eyes. The king had been wicked and was going to make my job so much easier. Well, as long as they truly were at their breaking point.

I needed the people to start a revolt. Without their unknowing help, things would get a lot messier.

A throat cleared. "Miss Justad, it's your turn."

Damn, the security had come a long way in three

years. My picture had already been shared with the other guards. Maybe this wouldn't be as easy as I thought.

I pretended to drop my bucket. "Oh my. I'm sorry. It's been a long trip to get here. I just needed some water for my parched throat."

The bastards didn't even offer to help. Though, it worked for me. I pulled one vial from my pants and poured it into the bucket before I stood back up. If I couldn't dump the contents directly into the well, I'd have to be creative.

He watched my every move as I dropped the bucket into the well and brought it back up. "Well, that's just too much for me to drink on my own." I blushed at the guard and poured the water back in, hopefully along with the poison.

He grunted. "Your bucket is empty again. Please refill it and move on before we have to ask you to leave."

I gave him a meek smile and did just that before striding toward the market. The area was placed just in front of the castle, and I didn't hide my attempts to gawk at the structure. Considering I was supposed to be visiting, it would only be normal.

The entire area, including the castle and market, was surrounded by a brick exterior wall that had been there since before I was born. But what was new was the secondary wall separating the castle from everything else, using the same brick material. Though, they didn't stop with the wall; there were also barbed wires running up and over the barrier that I was certain wouldn't feel good to tangle with.

After I took in the new addition, I watched the guards. There were dozens of them spread along the castle wall, another six walking the public areas, and I spotted an additional four just beyond the entrance to the castle. More than twenty fae stood in my way of getting to the king, but hopefully that wouldn't be the case after I was finished with all the phases of my plan.

Moving along, I smiled politely at the fae behind their tables selling fresh goods and items. They each wore worry lines that they tried to hide with smiles, and guilt assaulted me that I used to be the cause of their concerns.

My head shook. No, I wouldn't have sympathy for them. They could have stood up to the king long ago. These people had made their choice, and now I was making mine.

Striding up to the first bread station I found, I made sure to use my accent again and convinced the fae to show me how he made his bread.

"Of course, just come around the table," he offered after I showed my curiosity.

With the secondary vial in hand, I waited until his back was to me before I turned around and sprinkled several drops of the bottle over the bread on the table. Then, as I tucked the poison away, I brought my hands to my head and swayed a little. "Oh, you'll have to excuse me. I must go sit down."

I didn't let him reply before I ventured back into the walkway and headed toward my next mark. First was the bread, then I'd find the fruits and vegetables before using whatever I had left over on the dairy. Thankfully, with this poison, a little went a long way.

This was the third time I'd used it for various reasons, and the results had always been satisfactory. The only disappointing part this time was that I wouldn't be around to witness the effects in person.

The next table I found was manned by two older women arguing over whose husband was worse than the other's. They had the produce I was looking for and didn't give me a second glance as I pretended to inspect the melons.

"And the toilet seat! He knows I have a small bladder and go to the bathroom at all hours of the night. If I fall in one more time, he's going to be missing some body parts," the blonde complained.

"Oh, you think that's bad? What about the empty jars of food? Every time I go to get milk, it's gone! The ungrateful bastard doesn't ever offer to fill it either. It's not like the heifer is a mile away."

I snickered as I finished the job. Gods, those women had no clue about real world problems.

After stopping at five more tables, I'd emptied the vial. It was time to head back to Finn's farm. I turned to leave, and the same guard who'd allowed me through the gate approached.

He eyed my arms. "You've been here for over an hour, and you've bought nothing. Why is that?"

"Well, you must have missed me earlier when I'd eaten a lovely salad from Serene two aisles down, and if you'd like to check with the guards at the well, I'm sure they'll remember I was there for water. My trip home is long, and I can't bring items with me. My visit this time was purely for finding my heritage again. I intend to come back and make a longer stay now that I know the grief won't drown me when visiting the last place my parents were alive."

I rambled, maintaining my sweet British accent and smiling up at the guard whose face wasn't nearly as nice to look at as Finn's.

I groaned internally. Where had that thought come from? I would not mix business with pleasure, no matter how delicious the darkness in him had tasted.

The guard appraised me once more, but I wasn't nervous. He had nothing on me. Unless the king had turned his men completely ruthless, I was walking out of the marketplace of my own accord.

"Where are you headed now?" he asked.

I raised a brow, showing the real me for the first time all afternoon. "Why? Are you inviting me somewhere?"

He choked and sputtered. "I-you… No, miss. I wasn't."

This fae had no idea how to handle a real woman.

"Disappointing. Well, maybe I'll see you next time I visit." I patted him on the chest, successfully avoiding having to weave more lies into my story, and brushed against him as I passed by, heading toward the gate.

Exiting the compound was almost too easy. That was until I glanced back one last time and my eyes met that of my worst enemy.

King Easton Zephyr stood in the middle of the market, his familiar shit-brown eyes glaring at me as the guard I'd just flirted with babbled on, likely about me.

I wasn't ready to face the king, but I did take an extra second to soak in the changes he'd gone through over the last three years. I wouldn't have thought he'd willingly go through the motions of transitioning to the After Years stage, but there were grey streaks through his previously flawless auburn hair and wrinkles not only around his eyes, but forehead and mouth, too. Gone was the strong man I once feared, and in his place was a stranger I still hoped to kill.

All of the extra security suddenly made more sense.

Whoever had poisoned the bastard had shaken the king to his core. He was clearly already paranoid, and I couldn't wait to push him over the edge.

CHAPTER 16

When I arrived back at the farm, already having removed my glamor, Finn and Neva were waiting for me outside. Finn held no emotion in his face, just a dead stare that had me nervous. Feeling nothing was worse than being furious. Neva, on the other hand, was elated.

"Where have you been?" she asked after lunging at me.

I patted her back awkwardly. "Out. Did I miss anything?" My eyes met Finn's, and I finally saw a flare of emotion, but I couldn't decipher what it was.

"Poor Ivy had an episode. The poison in her causes her body to go into convulsions when under stress," Neva answered.

Ah, the pissed-off vibe I was beginning to pick up from Finn was making sense.

Finn crossed his arms. "Yeah, she had one right after we realized you were gone, and nobody had a clue as to where you might have run off to."

I pried Neva from my side and waved my hand. "I told you I had part one ready for torturing King Zephyr. I didn't need help, so I went and took care of it."

"What does that mean?" Finn snapped.

"It means that small traces of poison are now all over the produce in the market, and the well has been contaminated." I glanced at my non-existent watch. "I'd say by nightfall, the effects will begin to show."

"How?" Finn said through clenched teeth.

I waltzed toward him and trailed my nail down his bicep. "You want to know my secrets, you better start telling me some of yours." I couldn't help myself from messing with him when he made it so easy most of the time. Even when I knew it was a bad idea.

Without waiting for a reply, I headed into the house. Maddox was just coming from the hallway, and his shoulders released some tension. "Glad to see you're back."

I nodded. "Do you have any business at the castle within the next couple of days?" I still wasn't sure I could trust him, but he hadn't told the others where I'd been, so I'd tread carefully for the time being and use him when I could. I had to remember he may have only kept my secret because he didn't want to get yelled at by Ivy for helping me.

"I could probably make a trip. Why?" he asked, and Finn brushed past me, waiting for the answer as well.

"I need to know how things are looking on West Island, but I won't be able to return myself. Finn doesn't seem to know when to bend the rules, but something tells me you won't have as much of an issue with that." That was the only hint he'd get from me that I saw past the sweet fiancé persona he put on around the others.

He grinned. "I don't bend the rules. I'm just better at keeping my temper in check. I'll make my way there tomorrow after I've tended to my own land. Speaking of, my day hasn't gone quite how I planned. I need to get back." He turned toward Finn. "Ivy is sleeping. Probably best to leave her that way for as long as she's able. She'll want to see Lucinda when she wakes as well."

Finn grumbled, but I stopped listening. Instead, I went to my chair and took a seat. It had been a productive day, and I was ready to relax while I awaited news of phase one.

Except, every time I closed my eyes to do just that, all I saw was the king staring back at me.

THE FIRST TIME MADDOX TRIED TO GO INSIDE THE marketplace, he was turned away unless he had something to offer the people. So, when we'd sent him back the following day with one of his workers, we made sure he had plenty to offer, including several crates of lettuce, corn, and fresh water.

He had been gone for three hours, and I was bouncing on my toes waiting for him to get back. Not because I worried for him, but because I needed to know how King Zephyr was reacting, along with the other fae. The whole point of phase one was to make the people second-guess the king's ability to keep them safe. I needed them to question everything.

Gods, how I wished I could have gone myself, but with their heightened security, my attempts at sneaking in would have to be few and far between.

"Ms. Lucinda?" Neva said from across the room.

"Yeah?"

She pointed at me. "I think Beatrix's spell is beginning to wear off. I can feel your magic from over here."

I glanced down and saw the swirls of teal dancing around my body and following my curves. Well, at least I'd made it close to the castle once without being outed. Now that I thought about it, the guard who let me in shouldn't have even known I was a dark fae. The spell must have been lifting even then.

I called my magic back to me and stuffed it down. If the block was gone and I used my power, then there was a good chance the king's guards would find me quicker than I was hoping for.

"What does that mean?" Finn asked.

"If anyone is looking for me and is familiar with my brand of magic, then they'll be able to find me. Let's just hope nobody thinks to search for me during the chaos." I winked at him and moved toward the window. Still no Maddox in sight.

Gods, I hated that I couldn't trust him fully. Ivy was doing better and swore he was nothing other than good, but she was in love. Emotions like that made people do and believe in stupid shit. It was why I'd decided to stop testing the boundaries with Finn. Well, as much as I was capable of anyway.

After his little show the other day, I had a hard time forgetting how he'd felt pressed against me with his tongue working its magic.

Finn hadn't mentioned it again and, since I'd been so focused on phase one, neither had I. Maybe it was for the best.

"He's here," Ivy announced as she came from the hallway. She'd spent a lot of time in bed and away from me at Finn's demand. Apparently, I wasn't good for her health.

Finn opened the door, and I followed him out. There wasn't a chance in hell I'd let him hear what happened before me.

They shook hands, and Maddox nodded to me. "I don't know what you used, but that whole area stunk like death."

"Are people dying?" Finn snarled and glared at me.

Maddox grinned. "No, but they certainly wish they were. They've got bodily fluids coming out both holes, and a lot of it is being dumped on the castle gates. They're demanding he find someone to heal them, but the king nearly killed all of the healers when he was sick, and the rest fled except for Ivy."

This was working even better than I thought.

"Did you see the king?" I asked.

He nodded. "I was asked to take the crates around the back side of the island so that they could be taken directly into the castle. Apparently, the king didn't want to share the goods I brought, and clean food hasn't been brought in for the people yet. Don't worry, though. I made sure to mention that to a few of the people I passed by before leaving."

"How did King Zephyr look when you saw him?" I needed to know that phase one had caused more than just trouble for him with his people.

Maddox shrugged. "He's old as dirt. He looked tired, but there was a bit of crazy in his eyes. He wouldn't let anyone in his room. Not even his guards. Instead, he came and inspected the food I'd brought and pushed it in himself."

"Good. That's very good," I muttered, wishing I could have seen it for myself.

"You're welcome for putting my life at risk for your curiosity," he added sarcastically when I checked out of the conversation mentally.

I waved my hand in the air and continued with my own thoughts as I considered when and how to make my next move. The king's foundation was weakened. I couldn't let him find a way to reinforce it before I acted again.

"If you tell me how thankful you are, I'll tell you what else I heard," Maddox teased, and my attention was back on him.

"What did you hear?" I demanded.

He shook his finger in my face. "I don't think so. If I'm going to help you, you're going to treat me equally and quit staring at me like you'd have no problem with killing me where I stand."

Well, if he wanted to be frank…

"Prove to me I can trust you and maybe I'll throw

you a rope, but I don't know you and you like to disappear to your 'farm' more than I think is necessary if you have other fae working the lands, which you should if you're any good at what you do. How am I to know I didn't kill one of your family members when I was last here and you're just biding time until you can exact your revenge? I'm fully aware I have unknown enemies all over these lands."

Maddox considered my words, and I caught Finn staring at me. There was something different about the glint in his silver eyes, as if something between us was slowly changing. At least on his end. Though, I didn't know what it was, nor did I want to. I reminded myself to remain on task once again, and I'd keep doing so until the thought stuck.

"Your reasoning makes sense, but still, if you want my continued help, you're going to have to do something for me," Maddox finally replied.

I raised a brow. "Well, I already promised to kill King Zephyr. What else is there?"

"I want you to send Neva back to Earth to find someone to heal Ivy. You don't need her here."

Maddox was right that I didn't exactly *need* her, but it was nice to have her around. Then, I wondered if there was a reason that he was trying to get me all on my own without any help. I trusted Neva. She was the only supernatural I probably ever had. I wasn't sure I wanted to send her away.

"There is no negotiating here, Lucinda. You either do this or you'll never get the chance to see the king's death through," Maddox added when I didn't respond.

I glanced at Finn, but he didn't say anything. I didn't necessarily need their help to accomplish my task, but if I wanted to be breathing by the time I was done, I probably shouldn't be such a stubborn fae, either.

"Fine. Neva will go to Earth, but she'll need to take some of Ivy's blood before she goes, and you'll need to start spilling everything you know," I replied.

"Deal." Maddox held his hand out and I glared at it. "My fingers aren't going to bite you," he added.

"I'm not so sure about that, but if you do, I won't hesitate to slice your head off with my wings," I said with a smile.

Maddox returned my grin. "I know."

We shook hands, and Finn huffed. He didn't seem to enjoy that not everyone hated me. Too bad for him.

"So, the king is convinced he knows who poisoned the people," Maddox said.

Shit. We'd made eye contact. Had he seen through my glamor? Had Beatrix's spell weakened at just the wrong time? With my slight panic, my wings unfurled and hardened as I waited for Maddox to continue, focusing on my breathing.

"He thinks it's the Renegades."

My brows pinched. "What the hell are the Renegades?"

Finn laughed, deep and loud. A sound I'd yet to hear come from his lips. While a glare formed on my face, I also had to ignore the way the sound made my stomach do weird things I'd been trying to avoid for the last couple of days.

"What's so funny?" I snapped.

Maddox shook his head, shoving Finn's shoulder. "Not funny, just surprising. The Renegades have been around for a while, but their numbers are growing. The king calls them anarchists and has wanted them dead for many years. I assumed you would have hunted them at some point."

I shrugged. "When you're told to do this or die, you don't usually ask too many questions." Both of their faces softened, and that pissed me off. "I didn't say that for sympathy, assholes. Just tell me who these people are."

Finn's face lost all joy at my lack of knowledge as he spoke next. "They're a group of fae who have fought against the monarchy for decades. Even when the queen ruled. We think they're the ones who poisoned the king, but they never admitted to it. They were quiet for a long time until three years ago."

Interesting that they didn't begin to act again until after I left.

"Wouldn't that have been something to tell me?" I asked.

Maddox backed up before Finn could answer. "I'm going to let the two of you sort this out while I check in with Ivy. She's staring out the window."

I didn't move my glare from Finn, still waiting for his answer.

"I assumed you knew. Especially when you were so ready to kill the one who showed up here," Finn replied with a sigh, and I was even more furious.

"The fae who killed himself? You knew he wasn't a

guard? I thought you said you didn't know him." Darkness bubbled just beneath the surface as I remembered the interactions with that fae and all that was said. "Do you work with the Renegades?"

The fae had accused Finn of turning on his people. I hadn't thought too much of it previously, but now it was making more sense.

"No, I've never worked with them, but I sought out their help for Ivy. They wouldn't do anything about her situation, but they've been checking on me occasionally since then."

My shoulders shook. "That would have been good to know."

"But then, that would have taken all our fun away," a voice sounded, but there was nobody else around us as we stood in front of the house.

Without hesitation, I channeled magic and sent a wave of it around the open area until there was a ripple and another fae came into view.

One I'd believed was long ago dead.

CHAPTER 17

It shouldn't be possible. I'd seen his lifeless eyes staring back up at me when I was only twelve. I'd hunted him through the islands like the killer the king wanted me to be.

I'd taken this fae's life.

He was my first mark, and while I had no idea what his name was, I'd never forget his face.

"You want to make me proud, don't you, Lucinda? Well, you have to prove your worth. I've allowed you to use my resources and time to polish your skills. Now, show me you can use them. Otherwise, I think it would be best if we part ways."

"Whatever you need from me, I will do for you, my king."

He patted my head. "That's my good girl. I always knew you were special. Now, let's show everyone else what I see in you. There is a man who has been terrorizing our people. I need you to track him and make sure he can't do any more harm to our lands."

I was only just finishing my training, but I was smart

enough to read between the lines. The king, the man who'd been like a father to me, was asking me to kill someone. I hesitated, knowing it was wrong. Whoever the fae was might need to be punished, but murder seemed a bit extreme.

King Zephyr grabbed my arm, squeezing until I winced. "You're not going to disappoint me, are you, my sweet Lucinda?"

The king's words slithered their way through my mind, as well as flashbacks to when I'd sent feathers through the unknown fae's chest and blasted him with magic, all while tears trailed down my face as a young fae who knew better but didn't feel she had a choice.

"Hello, Lucinda," the fae drawled.

Finn glanced between the two of us. "Edgar. How do you two know each other? She didn't know who the renegades were."

I could hear the suspicion in his voice. He wasn't sure if I'd been telling the truth, but I never lied. I might omit, but I'd never outright lied unless it was to keep my ass alive, like when I pretended to be Maribel.

There were no cares left within me, so I had no reason to lie. If someone didn't like what I had to say, they could piss off.

"Well, you see, Finn. Me and Lucinda go way back." Edgar nodded toward me. "Would you like to do the honors of telling our story?"

My head lifted higher, and I refused to let him think he had a leg up in the situation. "I killed him without even knowing who he was or what he may or may not have done." My voice was flat, giving no inclination as to how I truly felt about my past choices.

"Well, you obviously didn't kill him," Finn muttered, his tone telling me he wished I had, and I smirked.

"Clearly." I sighed.

Edgar chuckled. "I'm not an easy fae to kill, but you were definitely the first to come close. You're actually the reason our group banded together again. We'd been docile for many years, but once I saw the weapon the king had created in you, I knew our people needed to do something about it."

"Pity you were never successful," I sneered.

"While that might be true, we were at least able to weaken the king, and that was just as great a victory to us as ending you might have been. I'd always wondered what happened to the king's pet guard and when my men saw you arrive on this farm, I knew we had to act."

I turned toward Finn, and he held his hands up, speaking before I could. "I had no idea they were watching so closely. It was only the occasional check-in that I was aware of before. This is just as much news to me as it is you."

Edgar took a step closer and my wings twitched to attack. "You killed one of my best men. What happened to him?"

It was my turn to laugh. "That was your best man? The one dressed in all black that I took out within minutes?" Edgar didn't need to know Finn saved him and then he exploded. The important part was the fae *would* have died in minutes.

Edgar's midnight leather wings rippled as he rolled

his shoulders. "Don't be fooled. I said one of them. You see, I have dozens of warriors just like him. All who hold a fury within them they've been dying to release for years. The king wronged us all, and if you're here to join his ranks once again, then be prepared to die."

Finn stepped forward, always trying to be the hero. "She's not here to rejoin the king. I would have never allowed her onto my property if that was the case. You know my hate runs deep."

Edgar nodded. "That I do, but it's never been strong enough to sway you to our side, and here I see you've sought out Lucinda. So, it makes me wonder… why did you ask for her help instead of ours?"

"Because you nearly killed me last time I did so," Finn snarled.

"You have it all wrong, boy. You just weren't strong enough to handle the spell and save your own sister."

Even I knew Edgar had screwed up, but the overconfident idiot hadn't seemed to think Finn was man enough to do anything about it.

Finn flew across the ten or so feet separating us from Edgar and tackled him to the ground. Magic flared from both of them, and just as I was about to go find some popcorn and enjoy the show, more fae dressed in black dropped from the trees.

Of course, that asshole wasn't alone. Whatever magic blocks they had were just as good as Beatrix's spell had been, because I hadn't sensed a single one of them.

"Finn, watch your six. We've got company," I called

out as he grunted, exchanging magical blows with Edgar and surprisingly keeping up with the old fae.

As I approached the first two fae, I caught Maddox and another guy I hadn't met before, headed our way. Well, any help was better than nothing. If anything, they'd keep some of the renegades distracted while I killed them, one by one.

Without hesitation, I lifted my hardened wing, made sure my end feathers were razor sharp, then sliced the heads off the fae before they could even take one shot at me. "Who's next?" I cackled as fear shone in the other fae's eyes.

Maddox and the new guy were already facing off with two others, and I glanced back at Finn. He wasn't doing too well against Edgar, who was now on top of him.

I plucked out several of my feathers and sent them flying toward Edgar, but only one sank into his right arm; the others he'd just barely managed to roll out of the way from. That was alright, though. Even the missed shots had been enough of a distraction to give Finn the moment he needed to recover and stand up.

Four more of Edgar's crew tried to sneak up on me, but I already had more feathers prepared, assuming they had to be smart enough not to get close to me like the others. Before I could turn around, magic plowed into the center of my back, burning the shit out of my skin.

Wrath rose within me and I knew without having to see them for myself that my eyes were glowing with enough fury to star in nightmares.

The four fae stumbled as they tried to scurry backwards and regroup, but I shook my finger at them. "I don't think so, boys. You made your choices, and now you're going to deal with the consequences."

I launched into the sky as two of them began to fly away. My hands grabbed both of their ankles and jerked them back down onto the ground with a force so severe, the earth cracked underneath their bodies.

One of their heads was twisted at an angle that didn't bode well for his survival, and the other moaned while trying to roll over.

"You're making a mistake," the fae sneered as blood trailed from his ears and nose.

"No, actually, I'm not. I'm making a choice that will keep me safe." Without an ounce of remorse, I sent my wingtips through his neck and backed away when the job was done.

Finn was standing there, a look on his face I didn't care to decipher, because if he was disappointed in me for killing the fae who wanted to kill us first, he could kiss my asshole.

I glanced around, disappointed not to see the body of Edgar lying on the ground anywhere. He must have realized a dozen of his best soldiers weren't going to be enough to take me down. Unfortunately for me, that had been the smartest choice for him, but I would eagerly await Edgar's return. Next time, it wouldn't be Finn fighting him, either.

Maddox and the new guy approached before Finn could say anything to me about my choices in fighting style that would make me punch him.

"Several of them flew off when Edgar did, but looks like six of them are dead. Though, that only puts a small dent in the Renegades' numbers," Maddox said.

"Who is he?" I asked, pointing to the dark-haired stranger with Maddox. I wasn't a fan of new people.

"This is Dain. He picks fruits for both of our farms and gets them ready for market. His week at Maddox's just ended, and he came here to work today," Finn answered. When I didn't reply, he added, "I've known him since he was young. His mother was friends with mine."

I wanted to ask for more information, mostly because I never trusted anyone, but since Dain had jumped right into the fight without question, maybe he wasn't so bad. Though, I'd be keeping an eye out while he was here at Finn's farm, just in case.

"Well, Dain. Thanks for joining in alongside Maddox. You moved that little fight along quicker, though that meant I had less fun, so maybe I shouldn't be thanking you." The darkness inside me was thriving at the moment. I'd needed those kills badly, and power was flowing through me stronger than ever before.

When you follow your truest desires, you will have all the power you could ever need, my inner voice added after my own thoughts.

"Uh, you're welcome? I'm going to clean up and get back to work." As Dain's russet eyes shifted around the area, I grinned at the fact he didn't seem at all comfortable around me, and that was fine with me. There was nothing remarkable about him. Plain short brunet hair, eyes to match, and maybe six feet tall. The only things to make him standout were his nerves.

I watched curiously as he left with Maddox following, then turned back to Finn. I was prepared for his lecture about killing the fae, but instead, he shocked the hell out of me.

"Thank you for having my back and doing whatever it takes. Edgar is among the most powerful around here, and I've had enough of his crap, but I never knew how to do anything about it without the risk of dying and leaving Ivy all on her own," he said.

I waved my hand. "There's no thanks necessary. I just did what needed to be done. Now, you need to tell me everything you know about these Renegades, so I can make sure they don't get in my way."

Finn's hand rubbed over his shoulder where he had a magic burn. "Technically, we're all on the same side. All of us want the king dead."

"But they'd also like to see me dead, so let's not forget that. If you want their help instead, go for it, but I won't work with them. We can't trust other fae with their own agenda, even if their end game is similar to ours."

He raised a brow. "And you don't have your own agenda?"

"I don't. You know I want the king dead. You also know I won't put Ivy's life before that task, though I've given you time to get things sorted for her. And when I've accomplished my task, I'm heading back to my high-rise apartment where I don't have to deal with the dramas of these islands. There is nothing about my intentions that you're not already aware of."

Finn nodded. "I see your point. I've already made the mistake of working with Edgar once. I won't do it again."

I glanced around at the bodies. "We have more problems now, and I might need to speed up my plans. First, I'll send Neva back to Earth to find a witch for Ivy as Maddox requested. If there is anyone to save your sister, she'll find them. You'll just have to hope the elf succeeds before I do."

My magic blocker was gone. The Renegades knew who I was and could out me to the king at any time. Yet, I still wanted to screw with him and test his alliances before I faced him. If I was going to be fighting on his territory, I wasn't stupid enough to go in blind.

Edgar just might need to be a focus as well. Ending him could be cathartic, especially after him just showing up like he had any power over me.

Focusing on my own thoughts, I considered my plan and how it might need to change with the new information. My next step would be getting inside the castle, not just the marketplace. But first, I needed to follow through on getting Neva to Earth. Just like on Earth, I needed to remember how to treat my allies. I just needed to picture Maddox like I did the bouncer Gregory. It was all about give and take while keeping my guard up.

Finn was still watching me as I'd been lost in my thoughts. His jaw was rigid, but the twinge I adored wasn't present. "How soon before you move on King

Zephyr?" he asked, again surprising me because I thought his question would have been about Ivy.

"Well, there are a couple of things to do first. The first being that we need to burn these bodies. I don't know how Edgar survived my attack before, but I want to make sure none of these assholes get up and walk away."

Finn eyed the head of a fae with disgust that was only a foot from where he stood. "Word has it, he traded his life source to another supernatural that can bring him back from the dead. But I've never heard who he did that with or why. Rumors vary from witch to mermaid queen."

I laughed hard. "Mermaids? Really? Childhood stories are what that rumor is."

"And that's what the humans say about us, too," Finn countered.

"You really believe there are mermaids living beneath these islands?" I asked. I might not have been centuries old, but I'd never met another fae who had ever seen the mythical creature.

He shrugged. "All I'm saying is it wouldn't surprise me if the rumors held some truth, and whoever is keeping Edgar alive could be a problem."

That, he was right about.

"Come on. Let's clean up our mess." I sent a stream of power toward the head and fried it until it exploded, bits landing on Finn's leg.

"That was rude," he growled at me, but I could see a spark of mischief in his eyes and enjoyed that he wasn't looking at me with disgust after I'd killed someone for once. The real him, anyway. I already knew the darker sides of him liked me just fine.

Maybe this all wouldn't be so bad if we could get along. As partners and nothing more that involved emotion.

Then, he picked up a scoop of mud and threw it at my face. "Payback sucks, doesn't it?" His light chuckle was all I could hear as I wiped the sludge from my eyes.

"Oh, you're going to pay for that." The chase was on, and the bodies were forgotten about for just a short time until I'd burnt another hole through his pants, this time on the opposite ass cheek.

He tugged at his jeans. "Seriously? Again?"

I shrugged. "That other side looked jealous."

Finn smiled, big and natural. The action did odd things to my chest that I didn't like. It was one thing to want him physically and enjoy the passion his disdain for me created, but it was a whole different scenario to throw real attraction between us that held depth.

I had to step away. I had to focus on the task at hand. I couldn't let Finn be a distraction.

"We should probably get these bodies taken care of and Neva off to Earth," I said, bursting the bubble we'd been in for a few minutes.

His smile fell, and I pushed the guilt down, letting my darkness drown it out. "Yeah, I guess we should." He disappeared, and I kicked the head nearest to me.

Damn, why did I care? Caring was for the weak, and I was nothing of the sort.

Finn reappeared with a wagon, then began tossing

bodies into it. I helped him silently, that awkwardness between us once again present.

His movements were jerky, and I knew he was pissed at me, but that was better for both of us.

Once we'd loaded them all up, I followed Finn to a clearing behind his bunker and helped him dump the fae onto the ground. I did the honors of lighting the fire, knowing it would make him uncomfortable, then intensified the flames with magic until there was nothing left but ash.

"Let's see someone bring these assholes back to life," I snickered.

Finn just grunted. "I'm going to shower where the workers clean up. You can use the bathroom in the house." Then, he disappeared.

Yep, we were right back to where we started, and I should have been happy about that, but I wasn't. Not even one bit.

CHAPTER 18

*A*fter we were magically cleaned up from the fight and the bodies were taken care of, I went back inside to tell Neva what I needed her to do. I'd made a deal with Maddox and, if I was being honest, having Neva gone for a while might help me sort some of my shit out.

She had been enjoying calling me out lately, and with the mess inside my head at the moment, I didn't need her trying to force me to process anything more than killing King Zephyr. Well, now I also had Edgar to consider.

There was just too damn much at risk for me to be having some major life crisis. For the time being, I just had to remember that I was a survivor. If people didn't like what life had turned me into, then I had no cares to give them.

The me I currently was would be the only way to save the rest of them.

Hopefully Neva, Finn, and Ivy would soon realize that.

I walked into the house and found Neva and Ivy on the couch, faces stricken, clearly afraid of something.

"What happened?" I asked, taking a seat in my chair.

Neva was holding Ivy's hand and met my stare. "We saw the fight."

"And?"

"You killed all those fae," Ivy muttered. Gone was the strong fae I thought I could get along with. In her place was someone who acted as if they hadn't been standing up for exactly who I was during that fight.

My eyes rolled. "And if I hadn't, they would have killed the people you love most, then taken the two of you. Would you have preferred that?"

She glared at me, finally showing some of the backbone I was used to. "Of *course* not. I just don't know how you can sit there and show no sign of remorse for what you just did."

I leaned forward, answering honestly. "Because having remorse wouldn't have allowed me to keep all of you safe."

Her eyes widened as power radiated from every pore of my skin. I wasn't even trying to hide the darkness swirling within me at that point. The adrenaline of the kills was wearing off, and I didn't have the patience to deal with guilt being thrown at me.

Neva patted Ivy's hand as we both fumed, then gave me her full attention. "What are you going to do now?"

"Well, funny you should ask. I need you to make sure I have everything I could possibly need for the task of killing the king, and then I'm taking you back to Earth. I need you to find a witch for Ivy. Start with Beatrix and see where you get."

"You want me to leave you here alone?" Neva sounded like I was a child who needed to be watched.

"I survived on my own just fine before you arrived. I think I can handle the next week or so. I don't imagine it will take you long to find someone. Offer them anything but the apartment and Black Widow. I want this whole situation over as quick as possible."

She nodded, and I could already see her mind racing, thinking of all the things she'd have to do. Neva turned to Ivy. "I'll come see you before I leave. Just remember what I said. You're safe here. Lucinda won't let anyone hurt you."

Ivy glanced between the two of us and nodded. Her earlier feelings toward me seemed to have been dealt with, which made things easier for me. I didn't want to dislike everyone that was around me. I just wanted them to leave me alone.

Neva left to her pocket realm once again, and Ivy slowly stood. She nodded before waltzing back to her room. Maybe that was her way of apologizing for the minor freak-out over the dead bodies? I wasn't sure, but I didn't stress about it.

Instead, I stayed in the chair, closing my eyes and letting my magic ease the tightened muscles in my neck.

My inner voice was trying to break through my moment alone, but I refused to give it the power. Though, it was growing stronger by the day. Hell, maybe even the hour. While I used to enjoy the darker thoughts and often allowed them to bring me comfort with my decisions, this new pushy aspect of whatever lie within me wasn't something I was willing to put up with for long. I needed to figure out a way to squelch it soon, before it also became a distraction I couldn't afford.

After killing so many fae, the power inside of me was stronger than it had been in a while. I knew there was something wrong with that fact, but it was like the adrenaline rush was a refuel to my system. It allowed me to thrive and do whatever was necessary.

King Easton Zephyr had muddled with my mind for too long, and it had taken every bit of strength to beat him out of my head. Though memories still assaulted me on occasion, I'd come a long way and would never go back to being weak again. Not even to the darker side of my magic.

Killing the king would be the closure I needed. I would take it, and then shit could go back to normal. I'd go back to LA and forget this world once again.

Then, Finn walked in and my stomach fluttered at the sight of the late afternoon sun filtering behind him, casting shadows that reminded me of myself.

Gods, if only he wasn't so opposed to the darkness that swirled within him.

My head shook. No, not even then. I couldn't get

tangled with him. I needed to do my job and get the hell away from this place.

"Where is everyone?" Finn asked.

"Neva is getting the last of the items I'll need from her elf pocket realm, and Ivy's in her room."

Just as Finn went to shut the door, Maddox came in behind him. His eyes met mine, and I knew he had news I was either going to love or hate.

"What is it?" I asked.

"The king has issued a call to all capable fighters to join his army in hunting down the Renegades. He is blaming your little poisoning episode on them and is vowing vengeance as a way to keep the peace."

I raised a brow. "Is it working?"

Maddox's head shook. "No. At least, not on this island. Families don't like being torn apart by force."

"So, are we expected to go as well?" Finn asked.

"No. If you can provide much-needed resources to West Island, then you're exempt. So, we will need to gather whatever food we're willing to give up and bring it there with promises of more to come. Otherwise, they'll come for us if we don't deliver."

I laughed. The king was such an idiot. My plan was working even better than I predicted. Maybe he could even take care of my problem with Edgar for me. Except, I remembered what Finn had said. The fae couldn't die. Or he could, but he'd just come right back.

I pictured cutting him into pieces, burning them, and scattering him across the oceans. I wondered if his powerful friend could put him back together again then.

"So, we're headed to the castle?" I asked with glee. I could put phase two into motion earlier than planned if I could sneak back in with them under a different identity.

Finn glared at me. "You're not going anywhere with us. We don't need the trouble you'll cause."

"Maddox can glamor me," I said.

"And what about your magic? Beatrix's spell isn't working anymore, and there's no way you can keep that amount of darkness pushed down long enough to stay under the radar. The guards will pick you out of a crowd within minutes, even if they don't know who you are," Finn replied, and he wasn't wrong.

Damn you, Beatrix. I should have asked for multiple vials. Though, I hadn't anticipated coming to Fae Islands when I'd made the deal. I'd thought I was going to be ditching the fae and be done with it. That plan had obviously gone to shit.

Maddox was avoiding eye contact and getting fidgety. He knew something and wasn't speaking up, but that didn't work for me. I took a step toward him. "Spill it, fairy."

He snarled. "I'm not a damn fairy."

I sighed. "I'm sorry. All-powerful glamoring fae, can you change my magical presence as well?"

Finn gaped at me. "Did you just apologize?"

"Well, not earnestly, but the words count for something, right?"

They both groaned, but Maddox still replied, "I might be able to do something, but I can't promise it won't affect you in other ways. This isn't something I'm comfortable doing."

I waved my hand. "Yeah, yeah. I'm not worried about it. As soon as Neva gets back, I'll get her through the portal, and then she can teleport herself back to LA. Unless things have changed, I don't believe others can come and go without a fae escort?"

Finn nodded. "But you won't be able to do it unless Maddox can change you first. You only got through undetected because you had no magical or even human presence. If you go through the forcefield, they'll know you're here this time. Honestly, I'm surprised you made it through the first time. I'll take her like before."

I shrugged. "Fine by me. I'll stay here and go through the items Neva has for me, and then Maddox can do his thing on me."

Ivy pushed past me, glaring at Maddox. "What is this thing you're doing *on* her?"

There was the strong version of her I preferred. No longer did she seem afraid.

Maddox stepped toward her. "That's not what it sounded like. I need to disguise Lucinda, so we can go to the castle."

She held her glare, hands on her hips, and her foot tapping. "When do you plan on doing this?" she finally asked.

Finn glanced at the time. "A delivery at night would be suspicious. We're actually probably better waiting until morning."

Disappointment rushed through me.

Go without them. You don't need them.

Gods, shut the hell up.

And now I was talking to myself. Damn, I needed to get away, and not just from them.

"If they're so desperate for supplies, wouldn't a night delivery be appreciated?" I asked, hoping to change his mind. I would need Finn to get back in. I couldn't use Maribel again so soon, given that she was supposed to be from so far away and only visit occasionally. Plus, if the guards had been smart, they'd have combed through every bit of evidence for the day and made me as one of their suspects. Sure, they might let me into the castle again as Maribel, but I doubted I'd be coming back out if I tried.

"She has a point," Maddox said.

Finn shot him a shut-the-hell-up glare. "We're not rushing into this. We leave tomorrow. Tonight, we get Neva back to Earth and prepare what we need for the delivery." Then, he turned his scowl on me.

I held my hands up. "Don't send your wrath my way. I said nothing."

"But you were thinking it. If you leave again without us, you'll be on your own the moment you do. And by that, I mean you won't be welcome back here." Finn's face didn't soften whatsoever.

"Okay, Mr. Pissypants. Don't have an aneurism over it. I'll be right here all night long." Okay, that was a lie, but I'd be on the farm. I needed to at least go for a walk and get some space after learning about Edgar. I needed to not underestimate him.

Neva showed up then, another trunk beside her. "What happened?"

I tossed a smile her way from my chair. "Oh, nothing. We were just talking."

She grimaced but didn't say anything more about the tension in the room. "Is it time?"

"It's perfect timing," Finn murmured. "I'm taking you to the border. Lucinda mentioned before that once we're on the other side of it, you can find your way to wherever you're going?"

"Of course." She smiled, and her politeness grated on my nerves. "How am I supposed to reach you when I've found help?"

Finn went to the side table and pulled out a pen and paper. Once he was done writing on it, he handed the note to Neva. "This is my email. Just send the word ready and I'll meet you the following day at dawn in Sri Lanka."

She took the paper, reading the script before tucking it into her front pocket. "Very well." She turned to me. "Do you need anything else, Ms. Lucinda?"

"I need a lot of things, none of which you can provide for me, unfortunately."

Neva nodded, likely reading between my words, because she seemed to enjoy that so much. Then, she surprised the hell out of me by darting into my personal space and awkwardly hugging me.

My brain didn't even have enough time to register the gesture before she was already on her way to do the same to Ivy, but without the awkwardness. My heart stirred, but I didn't have time to ponder my own feelings. That was for after I was done on Fae Islands and back home in LA.

Finn walked past me and guided Neva from the house. "Let's get you on your way if you're ready."

Neva faced me one more time. "Stay safe, Lucy."

Damn her.

"Yeah. You, too," I grumbled.

CHAPTER 19

The following morning, Maddox showed up with three crates of plumcots, some interesting fruit hybrid I'd never heard of. I also hadn't ever tasted one and gladly stole a couple while we waited on Finn. Sweet juice trailed down my chin with the first bite, and I decided I would definitely be checking out Maddox's farm when this was all over.

Finn finally came from the orchards with Dain behind him, pulling a wagon of more crates filled with lettuce, tomatoes, and carrots. "These should get the king's attention."

I grinned. That they would, since I ruined every bit of lettuce at the marketplace. Having a salad for fae was like coffee for humans. The fresh veggies were an obsession for some, including King Zephyr. It was my main reason for destroying the produce.

"Are you ready for me to do the glamor?" Maddox asked.

"Been ready since yesterday," I replied.

His wings unfurled, thin yet strong, swirling with blues and greens. Then, he rubbed his hands together, creating friction sparks. "I'm going to do the magic dampener first. It will be harder than the glamor."

"Whatever you say." I moved closer to Maddox, while catching Dain standing close to watch. He was a young fae, probably five years younger than me, but it didn't appear he'd had the same torturous upbringing as I'd had. There was still an innocence about him that put me off. Almost like Ivy. Maybe he wasn't so bad and I was just overwhelmed from being around all of these people who were nothing like me.

Maddox stepped closer and placed his hand over my chest, then frowned.

"What?" I asked.

"Nothing. I'm just not used to using my power like this." He moved his hand lower, nearly cupping my boob.

I was about to call him on it, but he hissed at the same time a storm erupted inside me. My head tilted back, and I gritted my teeth. My inner voice was *not* happy with me.

Stop him. Now!

My arm flew up without my doing and punched Maddox in the jaw. The force was enough that I heard his teeth rattle, but he didn't release me.

"Lucinda, what the hell was that?" Finn snarled.

I clenched my fists at my side, ignoring the demands from the power within me. "Ask him."

Finn stepped back and pulled Dain with him. I

wondered why until I saw black swirls begin to dance around Maddox's hands.

"Uh, what are you doing, Fairy?" I asked through gritted teeth, still trying to rein in the darkness.

"I haven't a damn clue. Now, shut up while I figure it out."

Well, someone had woken up on the wrong side of the farm today.

Pain seared through my chest, and I ended up punching him at least three more times. Another hit to the jaw and a couple jabs to the ribs, but I had to give him credit. He didn't waver from his task, showing true strength I didn't often see in fae.

I'd really wanted to scream out in agony, but King Zephyr had beat the ability to show weakness from me long ago. Instead, I stayed tense and rode the wave, trying to absorb it instead of fight what I couldn't change.

Maddox finally pulled his hands away, took a step back, and threw up in the dirt.

"That's a little dramatic, don't you think?" I asked.

"Shut your damn mouth," Finn snapped.

Gods, he was testy this morning.

You will regret what you've done, the darkness whispered, fading away.

"Did it work?" Dain asked.

Finn strode closer, his eyes appraising me with a hint of the heated passion that I so enjoyed drawing from him. "Yeah. They'll know she's a dark fae, but her power seems about a quarter of what it was, and it's muddled with Maddox's, so it won't put off her particular mark."

The darker side of me bristled at his comment, but something else took over, stuffing it down further. A giggle escaped, and I covered my mouth before snarling at Maddox who was still dry-heaving several feet away from me.

A glee filled me as Maddox's magical scent lured me in, and not in a sinister way, either. My emotions were at war with each other, and I couldn't stop the giggles that kept coming out.

"Lucinda?" Finn called, but I couldn't answer him. My focus was on Maddox.

My feet moved of their own accord, and I was getting damn tired of losing control over my body. When I was within reaching distance, I began to rub Maddox's back in soothing strokes while he continued to be sick.

What the hell is happening to me?

I heard a murmur of a reply from my inner darkness that loved to antagonize me but missed the words.

"Are you okay, Maddie?" I said the words, but the voice that left me was not mine. The actions were not mine, either. Was this the side effect Maddox had mentioned? I was going to kill that fae.

"Finn, get her away from me." Maddox hobbled a few feet back and offended this new, hopefully extremely temporary me.

"Maddie, don't leave me," I whined, reaching for him again.

"Finn. I mean it. Right. Now."

Strong arms wrapped around me, but just because I wasn't acting sane, didn't mean I wasn't at full power. I retaliated, extending my wings, and Finn let go before the feathers could harden.

"Lucinda. Calm down," he warned.

"Don't tell me what to do, Finn." His name left my tongue in disgust.

Dain chuckled, and I hurled a ball of magic at him. He didn't dodge it in time, and I singed through his sleeve. Served the asshole right.

I turned for Maddox, and he was standing normally again. "Lucinda, listen to Finn. You need to focus on him and not me."

I pouted. Like, full lower lip and all. I wanted to punch myself in the vagina. "But Maddie. I need you," I whined.

Oh, my Gods. Kill me now.

Finn threw himself at me again when I was relaxed. This time, he was more prepared. He shocked the shit out of me with his magic and rolled us onto the ground with me underneath him as my wings softened. His fingers wrapped around my shoulders while his knees held down my hands.

I could have fought him, but as soon as I met his liquid stare, I didn't want to.

My fingers trailed up his thighs, and I smirked. "Why do we keep finding ourselves in this position?"

He shook his head. "Because you just might be more trouble than I ever thought possible."

My hand moved between his legs and grabbed on tight. "Is that so?"

Finn sucked in a breath. "Maddox." The name came out through clenched teeth.

"Give her another zap and she should be good," he replied.

My arms moved to stop him, but Finn was faster than my inebriated self. I bucked beneath the fae, my feathers becoming razor sharp once more as I finally felt control come back to me. Magic exploded from my skin, and I blasted Finn off me.

"What the shit, Fairy?" I lunged for Maddox, but Finn stopped me before I could cause any more harm.

"I tried to warn you." He shrugged.

Damn, we hadn't even left the farm. After all of the nonsense that had been happening in my head, I needed something to go right. My eyes closed, and I focused on myself and nothing else until my body relaxed and Finn let me go. "That was not okay," I said.

"But it was a little funny." Maddox grinned.

I glared at him. "Maybe in a few decades, I'll find it funny. But mention this to anyone and I will torture you for days before leaving you to suffer and die alone."

His smile fell away, and he straightened. "How about that glamor?"

"A glamor sounds fabulous. Just make sure it's different than before. I don't want to underestimate the king's guards' ability to figure out who poisoned all of their food and water," I replied, feeling calmer by the moment, now that I was back in control.

Finn stepped closer. "She'll need an identity to get through the gates." He turned to me. "How did you do it before?"

"I knew of a family that had died. I pretended to be their long-lost daughter that had been living on Earth."

Finn gaped. "They bought that?"

I grinned. "I can be very convincing if you haven't figured that out already."

He muttered words under his breath, then glanced back at Maddox. "I know you won't like this, but what if we make her look like Ivy? It would make sense for Ivy to be with me and Dain helping you."

Maddox groaned. "It's a great idea that I really hate."

Before I could have a say in it, he stepped forward and worked his magic again. This round was simple and had no side effects. I lifted my hair out in front of me, taking in the blonde. This was some shit. I really needed to end the king and get back to being myself again.

Finn spun me around. "Impressive. Let's go. We've wasted enough of the morning."

Thank the Gods.

Dain stared at me as he carried two of the crates from the wagon. "Would you like to take a picture?" I asked.

Maddox snarled. "Not a chance in hell."

The fairy was a little possessive. I liked it.

Dain moved past me, keeping his eyes averted, and I grabbed two more crates. Once everyone had their arms full, we took off. Instead of teleporting there, we chose to fly to see if there was anything new that we could learn.

Unfortunately, the flight over was uneventful for us,

but I could spot crowds forming on the beaches of the other islands we passed. The hunt was already beginning, and I couldn't wait to be on the other side of it.

We landed on West Island, finding an empty spot. Maddox approached me. "I just want to double-check everything is in place before we get to the gates." After setting his crates down, his hands created the magic sparks again, but instead of touching me, they stayed mere inches above my skin. He started at my head, then my arms, down my sides, and all the way to my toes.

"You should be fine. If they question why 'Ivy' has darkness, politely tell them they can ask the king. She carries far less than you, but, given she hasn't been to the castle since the king nearly killed her, it is a plausible reason," Maddox added when he was done and grabbed his stuff again.

Finn moved to my side. "Let me speak for you until we're past the guards. It will be more believable."

Oh, he knew how much I'd hate that. I could see the spark of mischief in his silver eyes. "Say one inappropriate thing, and all bets are off. I don't care where we are or who is around us," I replied.

He ignored my threat and we headed to the gates. When we arrived, there were three times as many guards circling the walls. This was good. I'd be able to get a better idea of what I was going to be up against when it was time for phase three. I wouldn't be sneaking in then.

No, I'd be crashing through the gates with everything I had, because by then, the king would be fully aware of who had been messing with him. Hiding was only temporary.

Finn and Maddox stepped in front of me and Dain. I kept my head up, refusing to act meek, but also staying far enough back that they would hopefully dismiss me. I was stubborn, not stupid.

"What business do you have here today?" a different guard than before asked.

Finn raised his crates. "We have fresh produce for the king. Straight from our farm and never out of our sight."

The guard typed something into the tablet. "Names?"

"Finn and Ivy Barlow." Then he nodded to Maddox. "Maddox Sims and Dain Burr."

More typing. More glancing at each of us. More typing. Gods, this was annoying.

"The king would like your shipment sent straight to his private kitchen," the guard said to Finn, then addressed Maddox. "You'll head to the sublevel and leave those crates with the house staff."

Both of them replied with curt nods before the guard moved aside. I was honestly baffled this was working. I hadn't expected the guards to be such idiots after an attack like mine, but maybe I hadn't been giving the food we'd brought enough credit.

There were guards every twenty-or-so feet, all dressed in the royal blue garb with their leather wings out and ready for attack. I assumed someone would escort us to our destinations, but with sentries standing so close together, it wasn't really necessary.

When we arrived at the castle gates, another guard stopped us. "Which one of you to the king's kitchen?" Finn raised his crates. "When you enter through the double doors, head left and up the first set of stairs. Kitchen will be four doors down the right hallway."

"And us?" Maddox asked.

The guard glanced back down at his notes. "To the left as well, but after the stairs, you'll take the first door on the right to head below. You'll walk right into the sublevel kitchen."

The double wooden doors, likely infused with enough magic to kill dozens of fae, swung open and we entered. My stomach tightened with sudden nerves, but I pushed them down into the box filled with any emotion that made me weak.

Inside the castle's secondary wall, there weren't as many guards. Unsurprising, given the amount of force it would take to break through the additional wall, but I had needed the confirmation before I could initiate phase two. A plan I hadn't really filled the others in on.

"I need you to change me into someone else. Someone in a maid's uniform," I said to Maddox while glancing around for others as I moved into a small alcove just beyond the stairs.

Finn moved his crates onto his hip and grabbed a hold of my arm. "Not a damn chance."

I jerked out of his grasp, rage struggling to rise to the surface, but Maddox's magic was somehow keeping most of it suppressed with my darkness.

"You don't get to tell me what to do," I snarled and dropped my crates to the ground, making more noise than I should, before turning to Maddox and wrapping my hand around his throat. "Do it now or I'll call Neva off her search and all this can be over."

Maddox's eyes darted from me to Finn and back again. "You wouldn't," he snarled under the pressure.

"Try me."

CHAPTER 20

*M*addox was a smart fairy. He nodded stiffly, and I released his neck. "Make it quick." My eyes searched beyond the stairs we were tucked behind. Still, nobody was coming, but I knew that could change at any moment.

Finn grumbled next to me, but I ignored him. Something I was getting used to after only mere days of knowing him.

Maddox did his thing, and I went from blonde to redhead in a few seconds. "There. New hair and outfit. I'm assuming you're not staying with us?"

I patted his chest. "That would be correct." I caught Dain fidgeting out of the corner of my eye. He was off to the side, seeming as if he was about to piss himself. "What's wrong with you?"

"There sure are a lot of guards around this place. Makes me a little uneasy, given I don't really know why we're here."

And he wasn't going to know. Even if we could trust

him, that didn't mean we should. The less people who knew about my plans, the better for everyone. "Just do as you're told, and we'll be good. Finn and I will meet the two of you back here within ten minutes. If the guards ask why you're waiting, tell them we're in the king's kitchen and they should leave you alone."

"What if you're not in there and they check?" Dain asked, his brows furrowed and voice strained with what seemed like concern.

I tossed a grin his way. "That's not really your problem. Let's keep moving."

Maddox nudged Dain with his boxes, and they headed downstairs. Finn was already three steps ahead of me going up, so I quickly grabbed my crates and caught up. "What's wrong, Finnigan? You seem to have your briefs in a twist again."

"That is not my name, and *you* are always my problem. You do whatever you want without any regard to other people around you. It's maddening."

I grabbed his arm, forcing him to stop and turn back to me before moving to the same step as him. The staircase wasn't wide, and our chests were nearly touching while we each held our supplies to the side. "You have no clue why I do the things I do. I was living a perfectly good life before you showed up. One that consisted of me helping other supernaturals quite frequently, actually. I'm not here for me. Whether you believe that is your problem, not mine."

He had a solid foot of height on me and lowered his head until our noses touched. "You're infuriating."

"And you like it."

His free hand pushed my shoulder until I was against the railing. Then, he stomped the rest of the way up the stairs. Gods, I loved it when I was right.

The additional thirty seconds it took to get to the king's private kitchen had allowed Finn to calm down, and he was speaking with a maid when I peeked around the corner.

"I was just taking him lunch, but let me get this to the walk-in cooler first," she said.

I waited until the maid disappeared through another door before walking in. "Why didn't you tell her I had more?"

"You're dressed like her, and she won't know you. That might have raised questions. Now, leave the food and go do whatever it is you have planned. I will only wait here five minutes, and then we're leaving without you." His voice was flat and face blank of emotion.

I had no time to push him for more conversation, so I set the items on the counter and grabbed the serving tray. Phase two was getting easier by the moment. I not only had a reason to visit King Zephyr without suspicion, but I also had the means to tamper with his food while using another spell I'd acquired in the past.

When I'd seen it in the trunk, I immediately knew I had to factor it into my plans if the situation presented itself. I had assumed I was going to be required to physically touch the man in order to do so. Now, that revulsion wouldn't be an issue.

I followed the hallway toward another set of stairs that led up to two more floors. When I got to the top, I moved off to the side and pulled the potion and a knife from my boot. Lifting the tray, my mouth began watering at the smell of potato soup.

Grinning, I lifted the spoon and took the first bite. Damn, I missed the castle food. Two more bites, and I was done. I cut the top of the potion off and stirred the contents into the soup before positioning the spoon exactly where it had been before.

Once the food was covered back up, I kept moving. I knew exactly where I was headed and all the turns to take in order to risk being seen by the least amount of people, but that meant I'd likely run into guards, so I kept to the main halls instead and strolled along with a smile on my face.

The walls were covered in armor, priceless artifacts, and portraits of the king for every year he'd been ruling Fae Islands. There were only ten of them, and I hoped like hell that there wouldn't be an eleventh.

The next hall held portraits of past leaders. I briefly paused at the previous queen's. Had she been just as bad as her brother, or had King Zephyr killed her? Neither answer would surprise me. A dozen or so paintings hung there—the last picture of each previous ruler—but I paid them no attention as I hurried toward my destination.

I didn't come across anything new until I arrived at the king's door. The old wooden doors that had been hand-carved were no longer present. In their place were hideous steel doors with wood handles and one small sliding panel near eye level.

Approaching, I kept the smile on my face and bowed my head to the guards. "Lunch for the king," I said without making eye contact. Maids were the lowest of low to the king. They were replaceable, and I wouldn't pretend I thought otherwise.

Neither turned away from me, but the one on the left banged his fist on the door three times. No noise could be heard from inside, which I found interesting. That meant nobody would be able to hear him scream, either…

The idea was tantalizing and had me filled with elation in an instant, but I hadn't come here prepared to kill him. The king was nearly immortal, and I wouldn't be foolish to think I could end him without a proper weapon to remove his head, or even the most wicked spell I could get my hands on.

Finally, I heard two locks disengage and the metal panel opened up, only the king's eyes and top of his head visible. "What?"

"Did you want your lunch, my king?" the left guard asked.

King Zephyr's eyes darted down to me. Knowing he considered maids replaceable, it wouldn't be of concern to him if he didn't recognize me.

"What's for lunch?" King Zephyr asked.

I was suddenly even more thankful I'd poisoned the food, or I wouldn't have had an answer to that question. "Something warm and soothing, your highness. Potato soup."

He grunted and slammed the panel closed. I took a step back, assuming that was his denial and I'd have to try something different, but then more locks began shifting and I stayed put. Still, the guards said nothing to me while we waited.

Time was running out. I'd already been gone at least three of the five minutes Finn had allowed, but I wasn't concerned with them leaving me behind if it meant I had my chance at making sure King Zephyr's sanity was about to be compromised. Even if I couldn't kill him without proper preparations, I could at least take this time to make him suffer.

King Zephyr stood in the doorway and waved me into his chambers. Proper etiquette meant I couldn't look him in the eyes, but it didn't stop me from appraising the rest of him once I walked behind him.

His hair had been more grey than brunet when I'd seen him from afar at the gate, but it was back to darker colors and there was a tight set in his shoulders that told me he wasn't as weak as I'd perceived before. He must be taking power from somewhere, and I'd need to figure out where before I faced him again.

He turned to take a seat at his desk, moving papers around before I set the tray down, and I couldn't help myself from meeting his sour gaze. "Your highness. I do hope you enjoy." There was too much thrill in my voice that he apparently took for sultry.

He grabbed on to my wrist, the shit-brown eyes I'd always hated appraising my face and chest, while I did the same to him, noticing even the wrinkles I'd seen before were gone.

"You must be new?" he asked, his hold cutting off circulation to my arm.

I bowed my head. "Yes, your highness. I'll leave you be to eat your lunch."

Even though I tugged at my hand, he didn't loosen his grip. "What's your name?"

"Sally," I replied through gritted teeth. If he didn't let me go soon, my cover was going to be blown.

"Well, Sally. Take a seat." He released me with a shove, but I didn't sit.

"I sincerely apologize, my king, but fresh produce just came in from a farm for you, and I must tend to it before it spoils." Gods, I hoped he could see reasoning in that. I was not ready to fight him and win.

He stood from his desk, soup still untouched, and stalked closer. "I can see you take pride in your job. You want to make me proud, don't you, Sally?"

King Zephyr was only a few inches from me by then, and his use of "proud" was a trigger to my defense system. As a young girl, I'd only ever wanted to make him *proud*. It had been so ingrained into me that, for a while, it had become my sole purpose for living.

But not anymore.

He raised a hand to stroke my cheek, and I didn't hesitate to grab a hold of his wrist like he'd done to mine and twisted until it cracked. "Don't fucking touch me."

He roared, but I wasn't worried. The guards couldn't hear us. "You ungrateful little bitch!"

"And you're a dirty old man who preys on the weak, but I'm not a meek servant who will put up with some disgusting tyrant." My knee surged forward, slamming into his crown jewels. Then, I used my elbow to thump the back of his head. "Have a nice nap, Zephy."

His body went limp, crumpling to the floor. I might not be able to kill him easily, but I could still hurt him.

The nickname I used to call him before he turned me into a weapon slipped from my lips without a second thought. It was the name I'd coined for him when I used to think he was the greatest fae to walk the worlds.

Then, I grew up to know better.

He'd already begun to stir, and since I had no weapon to kill him with, I headed for the door, slipping through without opening it far enough that the guards could see the king's body.

They said nothing to me once again as I made my way back to the kitchen.

My feet were moving swiftly, and I told myself it was merely because the guards would be on my ass soon and not because I hoped Finn was still waiting for me.

My five minutes had come and gone, and my heart sank a little when I entered the kitchen. The maid who was supposed to bring the king's lunch up was standing there sorting through the food we'd brought.

She glowered at me. "Who do you think you are taking food to the king? Duties are assigned, and you must—"

I quit listening and darted for the stairs. I had no time for a reprimand that didn't actually matter. When I made it to the main floor, I took a quick second to consider going back through the front doors or the back ones. I was a maid now and wasn't sure which they'd utilize more at the end of their shift.

Shit, hadn't a lot of the maids lived in the castle? I couldn't remember. None of them had been important to me during my time here, considering how often they changed. Now I knew why. The king was even more vile than I'd thought.

Just when I stepped to go left, a plan already forming in my mind on how to get out on my own, a hand reached out from the shadows, wrapping around my bicep. My feet tripped over each other with the opposing momentum, and my body pressed against a hard chest.

It wasn't dark, and my eyes immediately met Finn's. They were charcoal and piercing with rage. Something unfamiliar blossomed in my chest. It was warm and consoling and unusual.

Finn's hands moved from my arms up to my cheeks. "Did you do what you wanted?" I nodded. "Was it worth the risk?"

"Only time will tell," I answered, my voice doing weird things as my pulse picked up.

What the hell was Finn doing to me?

He gave one curt nod, then moved in without notice. His lips pressed roughly against mine, and his hold tightened around my face. Where the hell was this coming from? I had no idea, but my body was no longer allowing me to fight it.

My hormones kicked into overdrive, and all sense went out the window as I wrapped my arms, and then my legs, around him. He turned us around, pressing my back against the wall while the growing hard-on Finn was rocking rubbed against my core.

His tongue explored my mouth with abandon while one hand sank into my hair and the other traveled lower, first circling my breasts, then trailing slowly down my ribs before looping around my ass as his kisses slowed.

Finn pulled back, hands still stroking my various body parts. "We need to get out of here."

I didn't want to agree, because that was the first time either of us had let loose without darkness or malice playing a factor, but I knew he was right.

"Where are Maddox and Dain? I'll need Maddox to change me again before we can walk out the gates."

"Dain had to use the bathroom. They'll be back any second," Finn replied.

"Really? Is he a child? He couldn't hold it until we were outside of the walls where people wouldn't sooner kill us than let us wipe our ass?"

Finn still held me, but as footsteps approached, we separated and pushed as far back into the alcove as we could.

"Yes, a maid. Now find the wench and bring her to the king. He will decide her punishment."

I knew that voice. It was one I'd never forget. Gabriel had been nearly as bad as the king while he trained me.

"Yes, sir," another male voice sounded before more heavy footsteps came and went.

Finn placed his hand over my mouth as Gabriel passed by. He was just the same as I remembered:

blonde hair, broad shoulders, and crisp uniform, as if nothing could ruffle him. Once upon a time, I'd wished he would save me from the king, but I'd learned he was no better.

Gabriel disappeared through a door at the same time Maddox and Dain came running from around the corner.

I bit Finn's hand that was still placed over my mouth. "Don't you ever do that again unless we're role-playing."

He tried to fight the grin but failed. I wasn't sure what had just happened between us, and I definitely couldn't decide if I liked it or not, especially since I currently looked nothing like myself. Now that his hands weren't lighting my skin on fire, I had most of my wits about me and kicked myself for letting it happen.

As soon as Maddox and Dain approached, Maddox tugged me toward him without saying a word. Magic was already sparking from his hands, and before I knew it, I was Ivy again. Hopefully for the last time.

Without wasting another second, we moved toward the front door with purpose. It was time to get the hell away from this castle.

CHAPTER 21

The four of us arrived back at the farm, and the first thing I did was remove the glamor with a bit of my own magic. My neck cracked as I stretched and ran a hand through my indigo strands. Not being myself was almost torturous.

Our retreat from the castle had been uneventful. Considering the chaos of the guards, we were ushered out off the grounds once they confirmed our story of why we were there. Only one questioned why we'd been there for so long, and I'd spoken—even though Finn had told me to stay quiet—blaming some maid with red hair. And just like that, they'd let us go.

"What do we do now?" Dain asked.

Maddox was already halfway to the house. "I don't know about the rest of you, but I'm going to go see my girl, and then check on my land. With the Renegades around, I can't leave it for too long."

Dain nodded. "Yeah, I'm going to head home now, too. Unless you need anything else, Finn?"

"No, we'll see you tomorrow," Finn replied.

Great, it was just going to be the two of us again. On the way back, I hadn't been sure what to think about the kiss inside the castle. It had been raw and unexpected, stirring emotions inside me I honestly didn't think I was capable of feeling. These emotions were completely foreign to me, and I wasn't even sure if I was identifying them correctly.

Neva had been the only person I'd ever let myself care about, and even then, I held back with my attachments to her. I knew one day she would leave me, and I wouldn't let that crush me. I couldn't care that much.

But Finn... well, he was different.

Not that I cared for him more than Neva already, but it was different. He made me think and feel in ways I wasn't sure I was capable of after the mind games the king had played on me for six years.

Maybe it was the poison in him that drew me. I had no real understanding of what the Renegades had used to nearly kill the king, but if Finn truly did have some of it within him, I also knew I needed to be careful. I'd gone through too much hell to go backwards in life. I wouldn't let another man force me to believe things that weren't my own thoughts, even if Finn wasn't intentionally doing so.

By the time I'd sorted through some of the chaos that was my mind, Maddox and Dain were already gone. "Lucy?" Finn said.

"Yeah?" I replied.

"Did you hear anything we said?"

I shrugged. "Nope. What did I miss?"

He shook his head. "Maddox asked for a few moments alone in the house with Ivy. I told him we'd wait out here."

His eyes were back to silver, but the charcoal outline was getting thicker the longer he stared at me. Instead of responding to him, I turned to the trees behind us. I needed something to distract me that wasn't sexy lips or muscled abs.

I'd made a decision to not get involved with him. While the make-out session under the stairs had been more than pleasurable, it was a momentary lapse in judgement on my part. I couldn't allow it to happen again.

Could I?

I grabbed a pomegranate and cracked it in half, then tossed one side on the ground while I picked seeds from the other.

Finn had followed me and glared. "You're wasteful."

"Why do you seem so surprised?" I asked even though I'd even inwardly cringed at my action. It had felt forceful, like I was trying to prove how terrible I was just to make him leave me alone.

You are who you are, Lucinda. There is no denying that. Embrace the darkness, because if you suppress me one more time, you're not going to like it.

Holy shit. The voice was back and stronger than ever, making my skin crawl. The inner me usually made me detached, more at peace, but this was evil and not normal.

What the hell was happening to me?

Finn nudged me, asking a question of his own. "What did you do that was important enough to nearly get us caught?"

Thankful he wasn't asking about the kiss, I gladly answered his question. "Well, I initiated, and hopefully succeeded, at phase two of my plans."

"Care to elaborate?" he pushed.

The words were at the tip of my tongue to spill right now, but if I told him what I'd done, told him what happened, it would mean there was some sort of trust established between us. Neva was the only person I trusted. Wasn't she?

I turned away from Finn, pretending to pay more attention to the trees than him, and gave myself a moment. If Neva was here, she'd tell me to stop being so damn stubborn, and I'd have laughed at her words, but I'd also know she was right even if I didn't admit it.

Finn had proved himself trustworthy to a point. He'd had my back against Edgar, and he'd waited for me at the castle when my time had been more than up.

It wasn't like he didn't know I'd done *something*, so there really was no reason to be worried about telling him what that something actually was. That's right. It wasn't necessarily giving him my full trust, just filling in the blanks to information he practically already knew.

I straightened my shoulders and turned back to him, flicking my hair back. "If you need to know, then I guess. Well, as you know, phase one was to turn the people against him even more by showing King Zephyr isn't capable of keeping them safe. Phase two is all about screwing with his head. I slipped him a spell in the tray I took and, if he ate the soup, then he should begin hallucinating, well, any minute now."

"You really are twisted." Finn's lips fought a smile, telling me, for the first time, he wasn't opposed to something I did. "But, wait. What do you mean 'if he ate'?"

A grin rose on my face, and he was already shaking his head. "Well, I might have knocked him unconscious and left him on the floor before I exited his chambers."

His eyes bulged. "*Why* would you do that?"

"Because he tried to put his hands where they had no permission being, and I wasn't going to let that bastard touch me, no matter the consequence. He's done enough damage over the years. It was time someone stood up to him, even if he doesn't know who did it."

Finn's face tightened, and the twitch was back. He moved in closer, grabbing me gently. "What did he do to you, Lucy?"

I lifted my head, meeting his liquid stare without showing any weakness. "Nothing I couldn't handle on my own."

"Did he touch you?" Finn's voice was nearly a growl.

"Of course not. I might have been naïve back then, but I wasn't stupid. I would have found a way to kill the bastard then if he'd ever tried."

Finn let out a heavy breath, and he pulled me closer until my cheek was forced against his chest. His arms wrapped around me, holding me tightly, while I stood there uncomfortably. At least, I thought that was how I felt.

I couldn't ever remember being hugged. Sure, I'd been in a man's arms before, but it was never simply to hug me. My heart sped up, and I couldn't breathe, but not like when I was having the panic attacks before.

No, the longer he held me, the more I realized a part of me was enjoying the feelings he evoked within me. The embrace reminded me of how wrapping my wings around myself and soaking in my own power recharged me.

Though, my inner self was not thrilled with the emotions circling through me.

Don't let him in. He will only hurt you. Or you'll get him killed. I'm all you need, and you know it.

Guilt slammed into me. Something else that was new. Was choosing to get closer to Finn, even if it was subconsciously, going to get him killed? I had no idea, but a part of me believed the voice and I stiffened.

Finn began to laugh, unaware of the reasons behind my actions. If only he could hear inside my head, he'd never have asked for my help. "Lucy, it's just a hug. I'm not asking you to marry me or anything drastic."

Might as well be, I thought on my own.

I spotted Maddox exiting the front of the house. He nodded toward me, and I pushed away from Finn, something I knew I should have done sooner, but hadn't.

"Maddox is done. Let's go check on Ivy," I said, backing up several paces.

"Do you really want to check on my sister, or would you rather not be alone with me anymore?" he countered.

I didn't like to lie, but I also hated showing weakness even more, and to me, love was just that. So, instead of answering, I rolled my eyes and played the situation off as if I didn't have any cares by walking away without him.

Finn followed behind, his steps getting closer by the second, so I lengthened my stride as much as I could without appearing like I was running.

Just as I reached for the door, he spun me around to him. "It's only been a few days, and I know that I wasn't very… accepting of who you are at first."

Ha, that was an understatement.

"But I see you now, Lucy. Every moment, every choice. It all becomes a little more clear, and I'm tired of pretending like the moment I saw you back in LA didn't take my breath away. After everything that has happened, I'm very aware of how short life is. My sister has exactly what she wants right in front of her, but she can't have it—or doesn't believe she can, anyway. I don't want to make the same mistake of denying myself what I want."

His words slammed into me. If he'd been going for a shock factor, he'd nailed it, because I wasn't sure how to respond. There was no witty reply ready to come out. There was no rejection I wanted to give. Instead, I pretended to have no idea what he was talking about, because that seemed easiest. "I have no idea what you're talking about." I waved a hand between us. "I thought we were just having fun."

My chest constricted at the lie, the words hurting more than they should have.

"Don't play dumb, Lucy. It's not attractive on you. There is something between us, and I'm not convinced it has anything to do with the poison I've taken on from Ivy. More importantly, I can see you wondering the same things. Quit being so damn stubborn and running from everything that doesn't involve killing or hurting other people."

He didn't allow me to respond. Instead, he pushed past me, and opened the front door. I stood there a moment longer, glad I wasn't expected to say anything, because I didn't have any clue what I would have said.

Somehow, within mere days, Finn Barlow had figured me out. He'd seen through my bullshit and called me out on it.

Just kill him and be done with it, that sinister voice in my head snarled.

Piss off, I replied, pushing up a wall between the power I usually relied so heavily on.

It fought back, but I was stronger. I would always be stronger.

Entering the house, I heard Ivy speaking. "Yeah, I've checked the email three times now, but nothing from her."

Assuming they were talking about Neva, I wasn't worried. She'd only been gone half of a day, and this request wasn't something anyone would take lightly.

Anyone who did wouldn't be someone we wanted help from.

"She'll be most successful at night. Even then, she might need to venture outside of LA to find the right person for the task. It could be days before we hear anything," I said, plopping down into my chair.

Ivy took my words in stride and surprised me by smiling instead of letting disappointment show. "Did you enjoy being me?"

I wasn't even sure how I was supposed to answer that. I'd nearly mauled her boyfriend and didn't think she'd be too understanding about that, even if I'd had no control. Instead, I blinked at her, hoping she'd move to a different subject. No such luck.

Her lower lip jutted out. "It couldn't have been that bad."

"Well, given the side effects, I'd say it was." I shuddered, the memory of wanting Maddox for those brief moments not enjoyable whatsoever.

Her eyes widened. "*What* side effects?"

"Why don't you ask your fiancé when he comes back?" I smiled in return.

She paled, turning to her brother. "What happened?"

He glared at me. "Lucinda was just confused about what she wanted, but we sorted it out and nothing happened, I promise."

She narrowed her eyes, clearly not believing him, but managed to let the subject drop. "So, what do we do while we wait for Neva?" she asked.

"*We* do nothing," I answered. "I will count on our

trip to the castle today being a successful one and then begin dismantling the king's army, one by one. While I wait for that, I'll be looking through these trunks for something to kill him with." My eyes landed on the chests, hopeful such a thing existed.

"You're not doing this alone," Finn stated.

I raised a brow and cocked my head. "You think so? Well, sorry to disappoint, but that's not how asking for my help works. I say yes, and I get the job done with no distractions."

He raised a brow. "So, I would be a distraction to you?"

Gods, I missed the pissed-at-the-world version of him.

"Yes, you pretending like you know what you're doing in a fight would only get in my way." The voice had gotten in my head earlier, and I wouldn't be responsible for Finn getting himself killed.

"There would be no pretending on my part. *I* don't pretend in anything I do, unlike some," he snarled.

Well played.

Ivy stepped toward the hallway. "I'm just going to go to my room while you two sort this out. Let me know if anything changes." She took two steps before turning back. "Oh, and please don't kill each other. I'm pretty sure I need both of you."

Finn and I initiated some horrid staring contest as Ivy continued down the hall, neither of us willing to look away first. He seemed to suddenly be convinced he knew me. Regardless if he'd been close on some things, I wouldn't give in to the weaker emotions he was trying to invoke from me.

Caring for other people only created vulnerabilities, and I refused to have a single one of those. Finn could take his full lips, hard abs, and sinful eyes, and shove them right up his perfect ass. I didn't need or want them.

At least, that was what I would keep repeating until it stuck. I might not like to lie to other people, but apparently, I had no problem doing it to myself.

CHAPTER 22

The tension from that evening flowed through to the following day. Finn was still convinced he could change me, and I was still trying to make him see how wrong he was.

Unfortunately for me, there was a thin line between attraction and aversion. To top it off, every time I'd been able to bring that twitch back, I realized it only made me want him more, which made trying to push him away even harder.

So, I went with ignoring him as much as I could, but he was a persistent little shit.

"Should I send Dain or Maddox back to the castle and find out if the spell worked?" he'd asked after following me out to the orchards when all I'd wanted was to be left alone.

Still, I didn't answer him. Even though I knew it was something that needed to be done, I'd ask Maddox myself as soon as I saw him.

"I could go myself, but Maddox has more

connections than me, so he'd be quicker at finding the information," Finn continued and piqued my curiosity.

While I'd done my best to not think about Maddox being a spy for the king because he had been rather helpful, I still hadn't forgotten my initial reservations about him. He made the perfect mole by being close to Ivy, running a neighboring farm, and getting along with Finn. It was almost too good to be acceptable.

"He's supposed to be here this morning, so I'll ask him when he arrives," Finn added.

Morning? It was already past lunch time. Maddox was late. How had Finn not seen that as something to be concerned with? I almost broke the silence by pointing that out, but the snap of a twig caught my attention.

My wings unfurled without notice, nearly knocking Finn to the ground. He was slower to respond, but he, too, released his wings and stood beside me.

I held my hand up, so he would be quiet as I searched the area. Running footsteps were coming from our left, but given how far I'd walked into the orchard, I had no idea what direction that actually was. It could have been from the house, the neighboring fields, or even the beaches.

Either way, I pooled magic into my palms, ready to fire at first sight and going with my motto that it was better to act first and ask questions later.

"Finn!" Ivy's voice called out before we could see her.

He stepped in front of me, protecting his sister from my potential actions. "Over here."

The direction of her steps curved to the right, and she came barreling through the trees, tears streaking down her face. My shoulders tensed. Tears made me uncomfortable.

"He's gone," she cried, falling into her brother's open arms.

"Who's gone?" Finn asked.

"Maddox. He never showed up, and since I couldn't find either of you, I went to his house, but he wasn't there, either."

Finn growled. "You went by yourself?"

She stepped back and jabbed him in the stomach. "Yes, I'm not a prisoner in our home. I'm perfectly capable of popping over to his farm on my own."

"Had anyone seen him?" I asked, and Finn raised a brow at me.

"No, not since last night," Ivy answered while wiping the tears from her cheeks and finding her resolve.

Finn wrapped an arm around her. "Don't worry. I'm sure he'll be back before nightfall and will tell us what happened."

She shuddered and nodded as Finn led her back to the house.

Finally, I was alone.

Only it didn't bring the solace I had expected.

I was at war with myself and, without Finn there to annoy me, had no choice left but to face the things I could no longer ignore.

For a long time, I'd been alone. Even when I lived with my parents, they'd never really loved me the way

I'd seen other fae parents with their kids. While friends had birthday parties, I had more responsibilities. The older I got, the more that was expected of me, until I was old enough to understand right from wrong. Well, my version of it, anyway.

The king had an easy mark in me when he'd taken me in. I had so badly wanted someone to love me that I'd taken his twisted version of parental care and held on to it with all I had. Any attention was better than none at all was what I'd believed.

"Your wings are magnificent, Lucinda." King Zephyr was running his hand along my feathers. "You're such a special girl. I hope you know that. I will always take care of you, and I know in return you'll always make me proud."

My smile grew wide. "Of course, I will, Zephy. I would do anything for you."

His fingers grasped my chin, a spark of something in his eye I hadn't understood at the age of ten. "You have the potential for greatness. Don't disappoint me, or it will be your fault for the actions I must take in order to ensure the fae people are safe. I need you strong. Weakness will not be tolerated."

Tears pricked at my eyes as his grip tightened.

"Don't cry, Lucinda. It does nothing but make you weak. You are of no use to me if you can't be what I need—what the fae need. You wouldn't want that, would you? We have something special."

My lip quivered as I sucked in a breath, keeping the tears from falling. "Of course not, King Zephyr. I never want to disappoint you."

The memory made me shudder in disgust. When I'd

truly understood what he'd done and how wrong the grooming was, a large part of me shut down, and a new side came to life. A side that had kept me safe and gave the king exactly what he wanted. Though, my actions had also protected me, so it took a lot longer to see through his manipulations.

Then, I thought about Finn, the emotions he'd stirred in me and how he'd come along just when I'd been feeling like I needed a change.

Was he the change I was searching for? Was he worth the risk of getting hurt again?

I didn't have the answer to either of those questions. As I traversed the orchard, I tried to list the pros and cons of what it would mean to open my heart to the possibility that I didn't have to be alone for the rest of my life just to stay safe. Maybe I could trust someone to stand by my side without completely losing who I was.

Over the last few days, Finn had seemed to be more accepting of my thought process and how I viewed the world. If we could meet in the middle...

Gods, why was this so hard?

Because you know it's wrong, the voice I thought I'd blocked out murmured.

Did I, though? The darkness no longer gave me the relief I normally craved. Instead, I'd begun to resent that part of me a little more each day as it continued to grow stronger. What would happen if I could no longer control what resided within me? That wasn't something I wanted to visualize.

Regardless of how strong the darkness was getting, thoughts of Finn couldn't be suppressed. Nothing I had done as of late made me feel like I did when I'd been wrapped in Finn's arms. Even if I'd refused to acknowledge it until now, there had been comfort and excitement.

Those were things I hadn't had in many years—if ever—and with that thought, I had my answer.

If I was going to stay true to who I was, I couldn't run from what was happening. I needed to own the new feelings and face them head on. If I got hurt in the process, well, then so would a lot of other people and I would have to deal with that. I didn't want to be afraid of anything, not even something that could potentially ruin me.

Without realizing it, I'd already begun to make my way toward the house. I quickened my pace and was just coming out of the trees when Dain came running toward me from the back side of the house.

He skidded to a stop. "They're coming." His breathing was heavy, and I had no idea why he'd been running when he could have flown.

"Who's coming?" I asked.

"The Renegades. They're bringing an army right here as retaliation for the people they lost since King Zephyr thought they were the ones to poison the food and water on West Island."

Shit. I wasn't ready for a fight, but I wouldn't back down, either.

"How soon until they get here?" I asked, wishing Neva was around. She would already be grabbing what I needed for a battle.

"Five, maybe ten minutes?" Dain was finally

breathing normal again and straightened. "What can I do?"

The door to the house opened as we came out of the trees. Finn stepped out, eyes tired. "What's going on?"

"The Renegades are coming back with a small army," Dain replied.

Finn's eyes found mine, and instead of the resentment I expected for bringing trouble to his home, there was determination. "I'm going to send out a call. The Renegades might have their army, but they're not the only ones fighting for a better life."

I raised a brow, impressed he hadn't been standing idly by while the fae world went to shit. Also, curious as to why he hadn't mentioned anything about another group of people.

Ivy came out as soon as Finn slipped back inside. "What's going on?"

Dain began to fill her in, but I cut him off. "Dain, you should take Ivy off the farm. If she can't fight, then we don't need the liability."

I needed Finn to be at his best. If he was worried about his sister, I wouldn't get that.

"Are you sure? Wouldn't it be better if I stayed to help? I won't make it back before they arrive," he replied.

Ivy crossed her arms and leaned toward me, a fierce determination set in her eyes. "I'm not going anywhere without Maddox or my brother."

"Well, I hate to state the obvious, but Maddox isn't here, and I don't think he's coming back. I had a suspicion before, and now it's been confirmed. It can't be a coincidence that he is gone the moment we need him most."

She growled at me, getting into my personal space. "Maddox is not a traitor, and I'm going to prove it."

"Well, you can't do that if you're dead, so go with Dain and you can convince me of all the things after I kill a few dozen fae."

She took a step back, turning for the house. "Finn isn't going to agree with you."

Dain followed Ivy, but I didn't. She could go tell Finn whatever she wanted, and he could make his choice. I needed to prepare, and there wasn't much time left.

I went to the trunks, not exactly sure what I was searching for. There would be no need for spells when I could openly use my magic, but I knew I needed something special for Edgar. If that bastard really did have someone more powerful on his side that was keeping him alive, I wanted to test just how strong this unknown was.

Magically enhanced swords and spears came out first. Those wouldn't be necessary. I would be going for stealth instead of show. My fingers traced over a couple of daggers that could come in handy in a pinch, so I set those aside.

Further down was a ton of witchy stuff. Apparently, I did a lot more work for them than I realized. Then, I found something that might work. Palming the grenade, I tried to recall where I'd acquired it from. It could have been another gift from the witches, or maybe from the shifters.

Either way, I had no idea what kind of boom it would make, and I was curious to find out. Especially if the boom happened in the center of Edgar's chest.

"Ivy, don't make me force you. I don't have time to deal with one of your fits right now," Finn grumbled as she trailed behind him.

"It's not fair. You can't just send me away. I'm not a child," she whined.

Finn whirled around on her. "You could have fooled me." Then, he turned to me. "Did you find anything useful?"

"For me, yes. Take whatever you want as well," I replied before stepping back to change my clothes. My regular jeans and t-shirt weren't going to work for battle.

Ivy threw her hands in the air, sighing heavily. "Fine. Send me off to the middle of nowhere."

"Okay," was all Finn replied as he began digging in the trunks, tucking items into the deep pockets of his black cargo pants that I recognized from the first night we met.

"Argh." Ivy stomped toward the door where Dain was patiently waiting, staying out of the arguments. "Even though I'm really pissed off at you, I love you, brother."

Finn paused and took a deep breath. I could tell from the strain in his eyes, he was having a hard time pretending like separating from Ivy wasn't killing him, but he was smart enough to know it was the best option.

He stood and walked over to her. I watched in

fascination, taking in their relationship I didn't really understand. Finn wrapped his arms around her and kissed the top of her head. "I love you, too, Ivy. I just need you to be safe."

She nodded, and the smallest of smiles graced her face. "I know."

They embraced each other once more, and then she was gone with Dain.

I couldn't even begin to understand how Finn was feeling. I wasn't sure I ever wanted to. The interaction I'd just witnessed made me second-guess everything I'd been considering just moments before.

That's right. Why would you ever want that in your life? It only puts us at risk, the darkness said, but I ignored it and focused on my own thoughts. Sorting out things with Finn once and for all needed to wait.

With my mind back on the coming battle, I used my fae magic to fabricate my warrior's outfit into existence, replacing my regular clothes. It had been a long time since the material graced my skin, but it still fit me like a glove. The bodysuit changed from ebony to charcoal like my wings, depending on how the light reflected off the lonsdaleite stone. I'd magically embedded one into the spider's silk fabric I paid a hefty price for, and it made my suit nearly impenetrable.

My boots were made from Kevlar and had two pockets perfect for the daggers I'd taken from the trunk. Once I had those tucked away and confirmed my outfit was properly in place, I braided my hair and twisted the long strands into a tight bun that was secured at the base of my neck with a bit of my power. I didn't need anyone trying to yank out my locks.

Finn was done as well by the time I headed for the door. I reached for the handle and cracked it open. More than five minutes had gone by, and we needed to be prepared for an instant attack.

Power pooled in my hand, and I pushed it out the door, toward the forest, searching for anyone who might be lurking in the shadows. It was late afternoon and the sun was shining down on the trees just enough to give plenty of hiding places for the attacking fae.

"What are you waiting for?" Finn murmured from behind me.

"You might think I'm reckless, but this isn't my first fight. Always knowing where your enemies are is key," I replied as my magic began picking up supernatural signatures.

"Some of those could be friendly, so watch who you're aiming at," he added gruffly.

I sighed. "And how am I supposed to tell the difference?"

"Just stick to the ones who are trying to kill you, and I'll worry about the rest."

Edgar appeared in front of the house. He was there in full armor with magic already swirling around him. "I think it's time we finished our fight, Lucinda."

I couldn't have agreed more.

CHAPTER 23

I double-checked the grenade I'd found was still safely tucked into my side pocket before opening the door. There were nearly thirty of Edgar's followers surrounding the area, most of which still kept to the shadows.

"Would be nice if Maddox was around to help," I grumbled.

"He'd be here if he could," Finn said confidently as he positioned himself at my side.

Edgar stepped forward then. "Oh, Finn. You're aligning with the wrong side. Your death will be such a waste."

Finn held his head high. "The only wrong thing I ever did was ask for your help."

Edgar laughed. "And you don't think asking for *hers* was a mistake? She's made you blind, boy, but don't worry. I'll be putting you out of your misery soon enough."

I moved closer, ready to shut the idiot up, but Finn's fingers wrapped around my wrist. "Wait."

Instinctively, my hand jerked back, and I was about to continue out the door anyway until I heard thumping from above.

My head tilted up, catching sight of an additional twenty or more fae swooping in from all areas. Most of them had leather wings, though a few had gossamer ones, but what caught my attention most was all of them wore teal ribbons around their arms.

"They will fight for you," Finn whispered in my ear while I watched Edgar's face turn from shock to fury.

The new arrivals wore the color of my magic, but I was still stuck on Finn's words. With Edgar distracted by the new arrivals, I turned toward Finn. His eyes were full of something I couldn't recognize.

"Why?" I asked.

"Because even if you don't know them, they somehow know you. There's a reason I sought you out, and even though I fought accepting who you are at first, I don't any longer. You are worth fighting for, Lucinda."

He grabbed my face with both hands and quickly pressed his lips to mine, momentarily making me forget we were about to begin a battle that could get one—or both—of us killed.

Finn pulled back, a fierceness set in his face. "You are worthy." His hands were still holding my face, and he forced me to nod. "Let's finish this."

This time, he didn't need to make me agree. His words had struck something within me that needed to be dissected at a later time, but I wouldn't soon forget his choice of using "worthy" to describe me.

Nobody had ever done that, and I'd spent nearly my whole life trying to prove that I was. Not only to those I thought I needed acceptance from, but also to myself.

Finn nudged me forward as the new arrivals landed out in front of us, taking on the fae who were going to give up their lives for an insignificant piece of shit like Edgar. It was almost sad.

During Finn's impromptu pep talk, Edgar had already moved closer, and his power pressed down on me. It was the reminder I needed to get my head back into the battle. I had a fae asshole to kill, and nothing else could matter for however long that took.

As Finn and I charged forward, fae-on-fae battles began happening around the yard, in the trees, and in the sky. Nobody was holding back, and as Finn darted left, I knew he was leaving Edgar for me to deal with, likely because I needed it more than he did.

I stalked toward Edgar, drawing my power to the surface, fighting back against his own, which was building by the second.

Yessss, the darkness inside me hissed with glee as I dropped all walls that I'd erected to keep it contained. I might not have been in agreement with my inner power lately, but I knew I couldn't do this without all parts of me.

My wings were extended as wide as they'd go, and the feathers hardened until they became razor sharp. By the time I was within striking distance, teal magic spun around me, matching the fury I had on the inside.

Edgar lashed out first, his power striking hard and fast, but I was prepared. My steps didn't falter, and I returned the hit with just as much strength. We circled each other, both of us seeming to be appraising the other and taking time to decide each move we needed to make in order to have the upper hand.

Finn roared from behind me, but I didn't let the sound break my attention on Edgar. I had to believe Finn could handle himself. He wasn't a distraction. I couldn't let him be, no matter the feelings he'd torn from me without permission.

"Your boyfriend won't last much longer. I think I'll keep you alive just long enough to see him be torn apart, piece by piece," Edgar sneered.

I laughed. "Oh, how little you know me, Edgar. The only thing I care about right now is seeing your dead body scattered across the ground."

His dark eyes narrowed as I pushed magic from my hands, feeling the vibration of my impact as it slammed into his chest.

"It's going to take a hell of a lot more force than that to kill me, Lucinda," he growled.

I smiled in return, already preparing for my next move. "I was hoping so."

Feigning right, I kept my sole focus on Edgar and swooped low to the ground before spinning on my heel, allowing my left wing to slice at his armor, which barely even took on a scratch.

"Good luck getting through." He grinned.

Little did he know, I didn't need to get all the way through. I just needed to get in, and the area around his neck was wide enough that it wouldn't be a problem to drop the grenade in. Well, as long as I could get close enough without him getting a solid hit on me that would take me down with him.

While I was considering how best to make that happen, my wings snapped closed in front of me, saving my face from being melted off after Edgar had taken advantage of my fleeting distraction.

Damn, he had gotten stronger since the last time I'd killed him.

My shoulders stung from the impact on my wings, but I ignored the pain and pressed forward. Edgar dodged my attempt at slicing his head off but wasn't able to avoid the blast of heat I dumped into his shoulder while he was distracted by the feathers I sent flying toward his eyes and neck.

"I might not be able to cut through whatever metal you've used, but I can melt the shit out of it," I said as I heated the right shoulder joint of his armor. My intention was to take out his good arm, but apparently, the asshole was ambidextrous.

His left fist slammed into the side of my head before I could dodge out of the way, and power rocked through my core as he magicked a blade into his palm, slicing at my suit.

Thankfully, the knife didn't do any damage to my protective clothes, but I was still disoriented from the head blow.

"Not so powerful now, are you?" Edgar jeered as I backed up, trying to regain my composure.

Finn was now in my peripherals, fighting two of

Edgar's men, and even though his chest was bleeding and something had scorched his forehead, he appeared to be holding his own. Glancing the other way as Edgar advanced, bodies lay scattered on the ground from both sides. Edgar's team had the experience, but whoever Finn had called upon seemed to have the drive for survival. Sometimes, that was more important.

"Are you ready to concede?" Edgar taunted and lashed out, but I dodged out of the way. "If you do, maybe I'll let you live and use you to lure King Zephyr," Edgar called out as he moved closer.

My moment of rest was over, and I kept my wings pulled in close for added protection as I moved in, knowing I couldn't afford to let him get another solid hit on me.

Let's finish him, the darkness drawled.

For the first time in a while, we were in agreement.

"Nobody will be conceding today," I replied as I slyly pulled the grenade from my side pocket and lunged for Edgar.

His eyes widened at my move. Clearly, he hadn't expected me to come in for a more hands-on attack, but I was done playing games with him. It was time to see just how many times this asshole could come back to life.

His right arm couldn't move much, but his hand still produced magic I needed to be leery of. So, when I was close enough, my hands latched onto his shoulders, and I spun around behind him, pushing his head forward as far as it would go and dropping an elbow to the base at the same time that I shoved the grenade down his armor.

I would have rather sliced his stomach open and let the mini-bomb go off inside him, but hopefully this would be just as satisfactory.

Edgar grabbed hold of my wing and jerked me back around to the front of him. My wings cut at his hands, but he didn't seem deterred by the blood pouring from his grip on me.

"Not so fast," he snarled as he managed to tug me even closer back to him.

A sliver of fear trickled through as I fought against his hold that didn't seem to be letting up. I had no idea what was in the grenade and really didn't want to be within the blast radius. I cleared my mind and let instinct take over, trusting myself to know what to do.

My arms reached down and snagged one of the daggers from my boots. Without hesitation, I raised the blade and slammed it into his neck, cringing as his blood spurted all over me, but it had done the trick. His left hand released me in an attempt to staunch the blood flow, and I jerked out of the right one.

Edgar's hand glowed red as he tried to close up the wound I'd made while I backed up. Finn was close and breathing hard, so I pumped my wings several times, sending him and his opponent tumbling several yards away.

My eyes stayed on Edgar's, and I heard the click of the grenade at the same time he did. "What did you do?" he hissed.

I raised my hand, wiggling my fingers. "Here's to hoping I never have to see you again." Then, I wrapped my wings around me to avoid as much of the impact as I could. Though, I still peeked through my feathers to see the proof that the grenade actually did what I needed it to.

Edgar's body shook, and the ground began to quake until fissures appeared in the dirt. All the fae I could see from my spot began flying for the sky except Finn, Edgar, and me. I would see this through until the very end.

First, Edgar's armor started to crack until golden light shone through from the inside. Then, that same light beamed from his eyes and mouth.

Holy hell, why hadn't I known I had this? It would have been more useful on the king.

Then, for the finale, Edgar exploded just like I'd hoped, and I tightened my wings around me to avoid the metal of his armor from slicing my skin open. The blood and gore, though, I wasn't so concerned with.

Momentary silence settled over the farm as Edgar's army took in their leader being blown to bits. After what felt like minutes, chaos commenced once more, but it wasn't enough to have me worried. Finn's friends, or whatever they were, easily took control of the situation and began capturing as many of Edgar's army as they could. Those left alive, anyway.

I glanced around and breathed a sigh of relief that at least one of our problems was taken care of. I couldn't imagine Edgar was important enough to whoever had brought him back before that they'd spend the time collecting the millions of pieces that I'd obliterated him into.

I moved to go to Finn but was intercepted when a dark-skinned fae with a teal band around his forearm approached. He reached out to me, taking my forearm. "We've never officially met, but I'm glad our time has finally come. I knew you would be the help we needed."

My brows pinched in confusion. "And you would be?"

"I am Mosi."

My eyes turned to Finn, plenty of questions running through my mind as to how he had set all of this up and what else I might not know about, but it would have to wait for later. I was more curious about the fae before me.

When my attention went back to Mosi, my chest tightened at what my eyes were trying to process. The fae hadn't had his wings out when he approached me, but they were on full display now. Platinum wings unlike any color I'd ever seen before were spread out behind him.

More importantly, they weren't leather or gossamer. They were feathered. Just like mine, but also different, because he wasn't a dark fae. The magic pulsing off Mosi had the energy inside me warring for power, but I managed to keep it locked down.

"Well, Mosi. I think I'm going to need more than a name to know who you really are," I said once I had my composure in check.

He smiled until wrinkles lined his mahogany eyes.

"Yes, there is much to discuss, but first, we must clean up our mess here. My people will take care of the remaining Renegades, and you're—"

Mosi disappeared before finishing his sentence. In shock, I turned to Finn to ask what the hell that was. Then, a thud sounded from behind us and Finn's energy burst to life beside me. I swiveled around and let my fury soar like never before.

CHAPTER 24

King Zephyr stood behind us with Dain at his side and no Ivy in sight. Rage flowed in waves from Finn in the form of magic, allowing mine to rise even higher as I soaked it in. Dain had been working against us all along, and neither of us had seen it. While I hoped Ivy was still okay, I paid Dain no attention as I stared down the fae who had turned me into a killer.

I was not prepared to fight him, but I wouldn't bow down to this king ever again. The weapon that might have been able to at least hurt the king, if not worse, had just been used on the only person who hated King Zephyr nearly as much as I did. Besides the fact that I'd once killed Edgar, he should have worked on trying to get me on his side, not holding on to something I'd done more than seven years ago.

"Hello, Lucinda. It's been a long time," King Zephyr sneered, then added, "Or has it only been a day? You never were good enough at doing what needed to be done. Always too emotionally involved. Even after all these years, you couldn't help calling me *Zephy* and giving yourself away. Though, I will admit, you nearly had me fooled."

Gods, I hadn't even considered the consequences of the nickname. The name had slipped so easily from my tongue. Apparently, I was still holding on to some residual effects from the years of mental torment.

Kill the king!

The darkness within me exploded more powerfully to the surface than ever, and my wings widened of their own accord, nearly taking out Finn with their sharp edges while he was having a stare-down with Dain.

"What do you want?" I snapped, pissed the hell off that King Zephyr clearly hadn't eaten the soup and phase two had been botched.

He shook his head. "I should be asking you the same question. You're the one who came to the only place you were banished from. I'd like to know what made you think you could beat me this time, considering you'd failed at killing me before."

I seethed. "I never tried to kill you. I saved your life from that shifter you called a pet and you punished me for it."

Emotions were rising within me that I hadn't experienced in years. Emotions I'd fought hard to stuff away and overcome before they made me too weak.

Abandonment.

Grief.

Sorrow.

Most importantly, never feeling like I was good enough.

The king and my parents had all abandoned me for essentially the same reasons. The irony was not lost on me, even though I did my best to never relive those moments of my life.

My hands were splayed out at my sides, sparks shooting off them as I made the choice to unleash the hold on everything that I was. All it took was seeing King Zephyr's all-knowing smirk to break the last of my control.

The moment I began to slowly let go of my hold, so did Finn. He was headed toward Dain with a dagger in each hand, but I paid him no more attention. We each had our own battles to fight at the moment, and for me to win mine, I had to push all cares out of mind. Even for Finn.

"What do you think you're going to do, Lucinda? You can't beat me. All you've done is help relieve one of my headaches with the Renegades," the king said without a worry in his deep voice.

"I'm going to kill you," I said calmer than even I thought was possible.

The wave of power I'd been releasing was ready for full impact, and I didn't hesitate to unleash everything I had in me. Every fear, hurt, care. All of it went with my magic until I could no longer feel any of it.

Finn had already advanced on Dain who had zero fighting skills. I wasn't even sure why the king had bothered to recruit him in the first place, but he'd gotten lucky that Dain ended up with Ivy. Now, King Zephyr had something to hold over us.

Finn and Dain weren't far enough away to avoid the radius of the magical blast I'd unleashed toward the king. Finn stumbled forward, and it appeared as if the knife he was holding went straight into Dain as they crashed into the ground together.

Neither of them was moving, and I wanted to care whether or not Finn might have been seriously hurt, but King Zephyr was already retaliating, and I had to switch my focus back to him.

My suit absorbed most of the impact from the king's return blast, but still, my chest burned with the amount of dark magic he was yielding. Ivy might have saved his life, but she hadn't taken away the power the Renegades tried to kill him with.

"You turned out to be such a disappointment, Lucinda. When your parents begged me to kill you, I thought they were so foolish. Your wings held so much power, it would have been a waste to take you out with the trash. Or, so I had assumed. Now, I see they had been right all along."

I couldn't ignore his words. His mental hold over me was coming back, as if I was a child again and no time at all had passed. All of the years I'd spent telling myself I wasn't weak didn't matter. No matter my accomplishments, I was back to believing I was nothing.

No, we are not worthless. Get up and fight him. Show him what he created, the voice inside me demanded, allowing a renewed sense of purpose to fill me instead of the fear of that little girl I'd once been who only wanted the king's approval.

Slowly, my dark magic began stripping away everything I had been. Feelings disappeared, one by one, and not just the weak ones. Even my fury was gone by the time the power within was done shaping me into the fae I needed to be in that moment. A fae without humanity. A fae who only cared about one thing.

Killing the king.

"You're going to die," I said matter-of-factly.

King Zephyr cocked his head to the side. "I tried to do that to you for years. I have to say I'm impressed you finally figured out how to turn it all off. You always did care too much about the little guy. Too bad you're too late. I have no use for you now."

He snapped his fingers, and pinpricks of agony settled into my skin and along my wings, but I didn't stop my forward motion. While I mentally acknowledged there should be pain slowing me down, I felt nothing physically. I wouldn't let anything stop me from the goal I'd committed to.

The king's jaw tensed, the only sign he might be afraid of me, even in the slightest.

"You can't kill me," he said before releasing another wave of power, this one snapping a few bones in my wings.

Still, I didn't stop.

Instead, I lunged for him, my hands reaching out and wrapping around his neck as shock traveled through my body. He wasn't giving up, and even though he was the closest to an immortal any fae could get, I refused to give up as well.

There was no fear of death inside me. I only had one purpose in that moment, and if I couldn't fulfill it, then I didn't deserve to live anyway.

Our dark magic connected, and I got another taste of what had nearly killed King Zephyr. The power inside me danced around his, calling it forward, begging it to come closer.

We will take what is ours, the voice in my head cooed.

A small part of me knew that wasn't right. We didn't need anything from the king. We just needed him dead, but the dark magic quickly snuffed out any doubts.

"What are you doing to me?" the king screeched as his navy magic began to join with mine, and wrinkles formed around his face.

"Taking what is mine," I hissed, even though I had no idea what that was.

His arms surged forward, slamming into my chest, power rattling my bones and causing me to release him. "We're done here," he roared.

"We're done when I say so," I snarled in return, except he was too quick. He'd come alone and already had an exit plan. I should have known better when he appeared with only Dain by his side.

Finn yelled something unintelligible, grabbing King Zephyr's attention. I moved back in to attack while the king was distracted, but the stricken look on his face made me look at what had caused it.

Dain's head was removed from his body and Finn was covered in blood. I tried to be proud of him, and the emotions began swirling within me, but my inner darkness snuffed the thoughts out.

We don't need him. Focus on the king.

Before I could do just that, power blasted off King Zephyr, pushing me further back. "You killed my son!"

What in the actual hell? That information even gave the inner me pause right before glee took over at the anguish King Zephyr was feeling.

"This isn't over," he muttered before disappearing in a cloud of swirling magic.

The king was right. I was nowhere near done with him. Not as long as he was still breathing.

We must hunt him while he's weak, my inner voice demanded.

Finn stalked toward me, his hands wrapping around my shoulders, and then hissed when my skin burned him. "What happened to you?"

"Exactly what I needed." I turned, but he reached for me again and forced me to face him, this time using magic to protect his hands.

"Where are you going? What about my sister? We need to find where Dain took her." Finn was expecting something more from me, but he was going to be disappointed.

I couldn't help him or Ivy any longer.

My wings spread, effectively pushing Finn away. Then, with one snap, an unexpected gust of wind sent him tumbling to the ground. My left wing hung lower than the right, but I ignored the injuries and focused on what was to come next as I soared into the sky.

I had only one task left, and whether it ended in my death or the king's, I wouldn't stop until it was done.

I had to destroy the last of my demons before they could do the same to me.

~

Continue reading Lucinda's story in Dark Fae Freed today!

In case you missed it, this series is the first in my Mystics and Mayhem world. Join my reader group Heather Renee's Book Warriors for more information on this world or check out my list of books by flipping a couple more pages!

STAY IN TOUCH

Find Heather on Facebook:
Reader Group:
Heather Renee's Book Warriors

Author Page:
Heather Renee Author

Or by signing up for her newsletter:
http://smarturl.it/HeatherReneeNL

Raven Point Pack Series

A complete Upper Young Adult Paranormal Romance series featuring wolves, witches, vengeance, and fated mates.

Blood of the Sea Series

A complete Young Adult Paranormal Romance series featuring vampires, open seas adventures, and the occasional pirate.

Standalone

Marked Paradox - A complete Young Adult Fantasy fae story about a realm divided and one fae to bring them back together.

ACKNOWLEDGMENTS

After so many books, I almost feel like this section gets repetitive... LOL But it doesn't make the rockstars in my life any less important!

For my husband and daughter. Without your support and encouragement, I would have never been brave enough to create all these books!

For Jamie Holmes, my bestie and editor. I dream of our next getaway!

My assistant Michelle Fritz, your kindness is something I will always cherish. Keep being you!

Ms. Jane Catherine. You are a gift and I adore everything that you are!

My cover designer Jay. You make my life so much easier with your talent. Please don't ever leave me!

To the new friends I've made this year and the readers I've been blessed to get to know. I couldn't continue without all of your support.

Lots of love and hugs to you all!

ABOUT THE AUTHOR

Heather Renee is a *USA Today* bestselling author who lives in Oregon. She writes urban fantasy and paranormal romance novels with a mixture of adventure, humor, and sass. Her love of reading eventually led to her passion for writing and giving the gift of escapism.

When Heather's not writing, she is spending time with her loving husband and beautiful daughter, going on their own adventures. For more ways to connect with her, visit www.HeatherReneeAuthor.com.